A Christmas Love

To Brittany,

Thanks for the support 8

Nmyl Love

26
1 7-30-13

Printed in the United States of America

First Printing, 2012 Third Edition, 2013

ISBN 978-1477636626
ISBN 1477636625

www.createspace.com
www.amazaon.com

To my Mummy, who has showed me the joys of being a mom and what dedication to the Lord can do in my life. I thank the Lord for giving me the gift of writing and the help to finish what I started. To David who gave me a crucial piece of information so I could finish this book. To Marilyn, my Muse, who let me read to her so I could work out the kinks, and all my other friends and family for your encouragement and support. I love you guys!

"Adam fell that man might be; and men are, that they might have joy." 2 Nephi 2:25, The Book of Mormon

Prayer Is Always Answered
By Cardinal John Henry Newman

The time may be delayed
The manner may be unexpected
But the answer is always sure to come.

Not a tear of sacred sorrow
Nor a breath of holy desire
Poured out in prayer to God
Will ever be lost.

In God's Own Time and Way
It will come back again
And fall in showers of mercy on you
And on all those for whom you work and pray.

Chapter 1

"I love Christmas crowds," said George Hart's younger sister, Jane, as they stepped outside the mall. "But it's always hard to believe the year is almost over."

"You and the store owners must be the only ones who like the crowds," George said as he glanced up at the sky, frowning. "I think the snowstorm they've predicted is about to start. We'd better hurry up."

"I'll race you to the car," Jane called out as she started to run.

"No fair!" George yelled back as he took off running awkwardly. "I have all your packages!"

Jane just laughed at her brother as she slapped her hands down on the hood of the bright red jeep. "I won, I won!" she gloated, then laughed.

"Next time you can carry your own bags. Here, take these so I can get the keys out," he groused good-naturedly.

"You're the one who offered to carry my stuff, so it's your own fault that you lost," Jane said haughtily, then ruined her pose by smirking.

She took the bags George held out to her then said, "Hurry up, it's starting to snow."

They stored all the bags and got in just as the snow and wind picked up.

"We'd better get home before Mom starts to worry. Ever since Dad almost died in that blizzard six years ago, she hates it when I'm out in any kind of bad weather," Jane said. "I still feel bad sometimes because he was out in the blizzard looking for me after I'd snuck out. I don't think I'll ever forget how scared I was when I found out he was in the hospital and the doctors didn't know if he'd regain consciousness."

"I know. I still wish I'd come home that weekend like I'd planned, instead of going skiing."

They were both silent for the rest of the trip home, thinking about the consequences of their actions.

When they got to the house, George parked the jeep in the three-car garage. As he turned off the engine, Jane turned to him and put her hand on his arm.

"George, I don't think I've ever thanked you for helping me after Dad was hospitalized. You helped me so much in coming to terms with my guilt. I really appreciated that."

They hugged for a few seconds before George pulled back.

"What are big brothers for if not to help you when you need it? Besides, you'd helped me, too, to realize that there wasn't anything I could have done if I'd been here."

"George, Jane, get your bags and get in here. Doug and Nancy got here ten minutes ago. We're waiting for you," scolded their mom Cherish, poking her head into the garage from the house.

George and Jane looked at each other and laughed.

"Well, there's one thing you can say about Mom—she still knows when we're dawdling," Jane said.

In the living room the rest of the family were waiting with an undecorated eight-foot-tall blue spruce.

"It's about time you kids got back. I thought we'd have to start trimming the tree without you," Kurt, their dad, boomed.

"No way! You know I get to put the lights on first," Jane said with mock severity.

"Well, let's don't just stand here talking about it, Jane. Get started," their other brother, Doug, said.

After Jane, with Kurt's help, had the lights on, there was a free-for-all with everyone grabbing their favorite decorations and hanging them where they would be displayed to the best advantage.

Amid the chaos and laughter that reigned, the phone rang.

"I'll get it," Nancy, Doug's wife, called as she scrambled to find the cordless. She answered, and after listening for a few seconds, turned to George.

"George, it's for you," she said, handing the phone to him. "It's Pat."

"Hey, Pat. How's it going?"

"Not well. Mrs. Hagerman isn't happy with the layout that we presented to her. She says she wants you to redo the brochures for the resort."

"Did you tell her that I'm on vacation? What about Johnson? She's good enough."

"Yes, I did tell her, but Johnson has almost too much to handle already since you're gone. Besides, Mrs. H. insisted that you do the designs."

"Can't a man spend a couple of weeks at home without having to think about work?" George sighed, slapping his thigh in frustration. "How long is she giving us to come up with a new brochure?"

"She wants them back for approval before Christmas. She did say that she'd be willing to send her assistant, Alex, over to make sure we get this done ASAP."

"Is Alex new? I don't recall working with him before," George said.

"Yes, been with Mrs. Hagerman for about six months, but already held in high esteem by the old lady," Pat replied.

Something in Pat's voice triggered an alarm in George's head. The same alarm that went off every time Pat was about to play a trick on him. George pushed it aside to worry about later as he surrendered to the inevitable.

"Well, I guess if she's willing to send someone over here, I'll do what I can. Have Alex bring what we've done. Make the arrangements with Mrs. Hagerman and let me know when Alex will be here. You know, if it was anyone else, I'd just have you do the layout," George said.

"I know, but I'm the numbers guy, not a layout guy. Besides, since Mrs. H. was our first real account and our best client, it's hard to go against her wishes. Somehow that little old lady always has me feeling like a naughty schoolboy."

George laughed. Although the seventy-year-old lady was very sweet, there was something about her that was quite intimidating. Mrs. Hagerman was the owner of a five star resort near Lake Tahoe. She took every aspect of running her place as seriously as a general would a campaign, especially when it came to advertising.

"She probably already has the plane ticket for Alex booked," Pat said.

"Wouldn't surprise me," he said. "I'll talk with you later. Take care."

After he hung up, he set the phone down on the baby grand piano that was his mother's pride and joy. When he told everyone what had happened, they were all sympathetic.

"That's too bad, dear," Cherish said, holding an ornament in front of her as she tried to figure out where to hang it.

"There was a time when a man's time off was his own," Kurt put in as he hung a garland on the oversized fireplace.

"I guess I'll live. It's not like I haven't worked on other vacations," George said. "And with computers, I don't even have to go back to L.A."

They continued decorating, putting lights up on the house and in the bushes out front, and hanging mistletoe from every open doorway on the main floor, all the while singing Christmas songs along with the CD player. While the family decorated the house, Jane took pictures of everyone. After she finished the second roll of film she pulled out a digital video recorder.

"Jane, don't you think you've taken enough pictures?" Doug asked. "You've done this every year since you got your first camera in junior high. I'm sure you've taken enough pictures to fill up a gallery."

Jane shrugged. "So what if I have? You don't know what great moment you might have missed if you don't have the picture."

"She's has a point, dear," Cherish said, heading to the kitchen to check on dinner.

At dinner Kurt blessed the food, thanking Heavenly Father for giving them an opportunity for the whole family to be together.

After the prayer George looked at his mom and dad, and realized for the first time what their love and devotion to each other meant to him. They had always shown their love for each other, and shown their children the importance of showing love for those around them, especially for those who were in any kind of need. They showed by word and deed that they *knew*, not just believed, that the Lord was a part of their lives, that He was mindful of all they did. It was this understanding and love that had helped him through some of the hard and trying times of his life.

That evening while Cherish worked on her Primary lesson for Sunday, the rest of the family started a game of Scrabble. George had just scored a thirty-point word when the phone rang. After a minute Cherish came in saying it was Pat again on the phone.

"Dad, make sure Jane doesn't look at my tiles, will you?" George said as he passed Jane, tweaking her braid and sneaking a peek at her tiles before she could cover them.

"Hey! I'm not the one who cheats!" she protested.

George chuckled as he walked into the kitchen for the phone and dropped a kiss onto Cherish's cheek.

"Thanks, Mom," he said taking the phone. "Yes, Pat?"

"I have it all arranged. Alex will be flying in tomorrow."

After George wrote down the flight number and hotel information, he asked if there might be anything salvageable from what they had already done.

"Well, from what I can tell, if you rearrange the layout for the interior of the ski resort, add a few more pictures of people enjoying themselves outside, and add your own pizzazz, you should be fine. But then, after you talk with Alex, you might have a better idea of exactly what Mrs. H. wants."

After hanging up the phone, he started to go back into the family room when Cherish stopped him.

"Why don't you invite Alex to stay here since you have to work? You can use your father's office, and not have to worry about anything. Besides, I'm sure Alex will be missing his family, and maybe we can help him with that," Cherish offered.

While waiting for Alex's flight to come in, George kept hoping that his stay would be brief. He didn't want to take too much time away from visiting with his family, especially since he was only able to visit every other year.

When the flight was announced, George walked over to the area where families and friends were waiting for the airplanes to disgorge their passengers. He held up a sign with Alex's name on it. As passenger after passenger passed by him, George started to worry that Alex somehow had missed seeing him. Finally he was the only one waiting. He was just about ready to go to a courtesy phone and have Alex paged, when he noticed a woman in her early twenties pulling a rollaway suitcase with one hand, a laptop case strap over her other shoulder, and carrying a briefcase, heading in his direction. She was slender without being thin, with shoulder-length golden-copper hair with enough curls to make his fingers itch to pull them straight. She was wearing a light blue silk suit that set off her hair and porcelain skin. As she took a few more steps, George realized she was walking straight toward him.

After setting the rollaway upright, she held out her hand and smiled. George's breath caught in his chest and all thoughts fled his mind. Belatedly he realized that this gorgeous creature was talking to him. Warning bells went off in his head as he vaguely recalled his unease while talking with Pat.

"I'm sorry. I zoned out for a second there. What were you saying?" George said, cursing his tendency to blush easily.

"I said I'm Alex. And you must be George."

George stood there stunned for another couple of seconds looking into Alex's chocolate brown eyes.

A woman? Why the heck didn't Pat tell me? Surely he's talked with Alex, knew he was a she! George thought.

At last George took Alex's hand. The sign with Alex's name on it dangled forgotten in his other hand as it dawned on him that this was a practical joke, that Alex wasn't a 'he' like he'd assumed.

9

"Uh, yeah. I'm George. I hope you had a good flight."

Alex smiled. "I've had better and I've had worse." After a pause her smile changed to one of amusement and she quirked an eyebrow. "May I have my hand back?"

Embarrassed, he dropped her hand and focused on the first thing he could think of. "Do you have any other luggage?"

Once they were on their way to the car George asked, "Have you ever been to Idaho before?"

"Not since I was really little. My grandparents on my mother's side use to live over by Rexburg, but when they passed away we stopped going."

"I'm sorry," he said with compassion. "I know how hard that can be. I lost my grandma when I was ten. We had a lot of fun together. She would come over for Christmas or New Year's and have snowball fights with us."

"It's okay. I was only six, so I didn't know them that well."

"Do you remember anything?"

"Only that Grandma always seemed to smell of flowers and cookies, and Granddad of horses."

"It's good that you remember something, even if it's only how they smelled."

By this time they had reached the jeep, and George took a couple of moments to stow Alex's bags before helping her in. George realized that Alex's skirt was just tight enough to make it difficult for her to get into the high vehicle. Before she had a chance to try, George lifted her and deposited her gently into the passenger seat.

Alex seemed a bit startled but did not comment other than to thank him.

"You're welcome. I've had my sister complain too many times when she was dressed nicely not to recognize when it might be a bit of a stretch to get into something higher than you're used to."

George shut the door before going around to his side of the jeep. He was just about to turn out of the parking structure when he remembered his mom's offer to let Alex stay with them.

"I just remembered. My mom wanted me to invite you to stay with us while you're here. It'll save a bit of traveling since you're set to stay in Taylorsville, and that's a half hour away from us. Rainsville, where we live, is so small it doesn't have anything more than a B&B, which I know is full right now. Anyway, Mom figured that it would be easier for us to work – we can use my dad's office – and you'll be able to be around a family during the holidays. Will that be okay?"

"If you're sure I won't be putting anyone out. I mean, you guys don't know anything about me, I could be a sleepwalker or something," Alex said with a small laugh.

"It wouldn't matter if you were a street person, Mom would still have invited you. Mom can't stand to think of anyone by themselves for what should be a time of reunions, friends, and family," George said.

"In that case, how could I refuse?" Alex smiled.

Alex pulled out her cell phone and the number for the hotel, called to cancel her reservation, and then called Mrs. Hagerman to let her know that she'd arrived safely and about the change.

After hanging up, she was quiet for a bit then asked, "Does your family go all-out for Christmas?"

"You better believe it! By December first or second the tree is usually up and everything is decorated, except this year it took longer to find the perfect tree. We bake cookies for knock-n-run plates, we go caroling, there's a Christmas party at church, tons of things." George grinned.

As he glanced over at Alex, his grin slid away. The easy-going woman that he'd been getting to know had gone. In her place was a woman who was sitting ramrod straight in her seat and staring out the windshield, a frozen look on her face.

"Want to tell me what's wrong?" George asked softly.

"Nothing's wrong," Alex all but snapped. "I won't mind staying, just don't expect me to help or join in. I'm here to do a job, not to celebrate the holidays."

Sure, there's nothing wrong, thought George sardonically, *only someone's being Scroogey. We'll have to see if we can fix that.* George grinned at the thought of trying to help Alex gain some Christmas spirit. How could anyone stay at his parents' house without joining in whole-heartedly? Love for the Savior was abundantly apparent, especially at Christmas time where songs of His birth were played from morn till night.

After a while Alex seemed to relax a bit, and asked how much longer they would be driving.

"About another hour and a half."

"Tell me about your family. I'd like to know something about the people I'll be spending the next little while with," Alex said, the ice in her voice gone.

For the rest of the trip, George kept Alex in stitches with stories of his family and growing up in a small farming community.

When they were almost home, Alex wiped the tears of laughter from her eyes, took a couple of deep breaths to calm down then said, "Boy, with all you've told me, I can sure see why you want to spend as much time with your family as you can. It's a lot better than what I grew up with." Alex clamped her mouth shut as if wishing she could retract that last statement.

George picked up on the change without even having to glance at her.

"What do you mean? Did you not get along with your family?"

"Never mind. I don't want to talk about it," Alex said sternly.

As they were pulling up to the house, George filed away the exchange to puzzle over later, his curiosity about this beautiful woman increasing.

It had gotten dark on the two-hour trip from the Boise airport, and it wasn't until he got out of the car that George noticed that Jane was in the yard making snow angels.

"What's an old maid like you doing making snow angels?" he asked.

"What do you mean, an old maid? I'll have you know, young man, that I am a highly eligible young lady not a day over sixty-eight," Jane said indignantly, carefully standing up and stepping out of the angel.

Coming around the jeep, Alex seemed to be struggling to keep a straight face as George kept the silly conversation going. "I would've sworn you weren't a day over twenty-one. You must tell me how you do it."

"Oh, it's simple," Jane said, waving her hand airily. "I just drink a mixture of all the creepy crawlies I can find to ward off my own ugliness."

"That makes perfect sense," Alex stated emphatically.

During the exchange, George had retrieved Alex's suitcases and stood there with tears in his eyes from the effort not to burst out laughing. But at Alex's last remark, he couldn't contain himself any longer. Once he started to laugh, Alex joined in.

"Oh, you think that's funny, do you?" Jane asked, as she quickly scooped up a handful of snow, making it into a snowball and throwing it at George before he could do more than take a few steps. The snowball caught him right in the middle of his forehead.

George shook the snow from his face and warned, "As soon as I take Alex in and get her settled, I'll be back. And remember, I always win."

Turning to Alex, George winked at her. "Come on, let's hurry so she doesn't have much time to get a bunch of snowballs ready."

Alex was doubled over because she was laughing so hard. She straightened up, took a quick breath, and headed over to the garage door with her laptop case over her shoulder.

Looking over her shoulder she said, laughter evident in her voice, "Yes, let's hurry. I can't wait to see if she wins."

George opened the door and let Alex step in first. He followed her, another snowball hitting the door just as he shut it.

"Mom, we're here," George called into the kitchen as they passed through. "I've a snowball fight to win, so you'll have to wait to say hi till I show Alex her room."

Cherish stepped into the kitchen.

"You will not wait till you've shown her to her room. I- Her? I thought Alex was a him."

"So did I."

"Well, are you going to introduce us?" Cherish asked, taking the change of Alex's gender in stride.

Caught out, George blushed lightly. His mother had made sure all her children had learned good manners, and here he was, flubbing up on something that should have been a no-brainer.

"Mom, this is Alex Johnston. Alex this tyrant is my mom, Cherish," he said with obvious fondness.

"Hello, dear. Did you have a good flight?" Cherish said, offering her hand to Alex.

Taking the offered hand and shaking it, Alex replied, "Nice to meet you, Mrs....?"

"Hart, but call me Cherish, dear, or Mom. With the children having so many good friends, we've adopted a lot of extras," she said, smiling.

"Cherish. It went well. Thank you for letting me stay with you. I don't much care for staying in hotels. As nice as they can be, they aren't a home."

"Our pleasure. Now you just follow this rascal and he will show you to your room," Cherish said with a smile.

George showed Alex her room, the bathroom, and the office.

"Go ahead and make yourself at home, we're firm believers in *mi casa es su casa.* If you don't find something that you're looking for, just ask any one of us. Once you've freshened up, I'll meet you in the living room and introduce you to the rest of the gang."

"What about your snowball fight?" Alex asked with a grin.

"Oh, well, Jane will just have to give take a rain check. Besides, if I don't have help, she just might win," George said with a conspiring wink.

Alex smiled. "Okay, give me about five minutes and I'll be there."

George quickly told her where the living room was, then left.

In the living room Kurt was watching his favorite Christmas movie.

"Where's Alex?" Kurt asked when he noticed George. "I saw a young lady with you. Who is she?"

"That lady *is* Alex," George said with some annoyance. "I suspect Pat is playing one of his jokes on me. He never once mentioned gender nor did he correct me when I did, and I know he had to have talked with her on the phone."

"Is it really that bad? I mean she's definitely not hard on the eyes."

"Oh, it's not that I mind working with a woman--in fact, sometimes they work better than men. I was just expecting a guy. You should have seen me at the airport."

"I didn't realize I was to be a joke," Alex said, coming into the room, a small smile on her lips letting them know she wasn't offended. "Is that why you looked so surprised to see me? And here I thought it was because I was so irresistibly beautiful," she said, striking a pose.

George's ears turned a bright pink and he rubbed the back of his neck in embarrassment. "Um, well, that might have had something to do with my reaction."

Now it was Alex's turn to blush.

Kurt laughed as he got up. He held his hand out to Alex and said, "You're all right. I'm Kurt, George's father."

Shaking his hand she replied, "Alex Johnston. It's nice to meet you, sir. Thank you for allowing me to stay here."

"There's no need to be so formal. Please, feel free to call me Kurt, or Dad, if you want. We're the adoptive parents to probably on the order of twenty of the kids' friends, so I'm used to it. We're also used to having a full house around the holidays. It's kind of quiet this year, so we're even more glad to have you stay with us."

"Thanks anyway."

"George, are you coming out for the snowball fight?" Jane asked from the doorway.

"You'll have to take a rain check on that. Mom already got on my case once for showing bad manners. I don't want to have it happen twice in the same hour. Besides, Alex and I should at least take a look at the layouts. Maybe tomorrow," George said.

"Okay. Oh, Mom said to tell you dinner will be ready in about fifteen minutes."

"Come on, Alex, let's take a look at what we're dealing with."

"Let me get my laptop and briefcase. I'll meet you in the office."

When Alex joined George in the office, she pulled out her laptop, set it on the desk, then sat down in the desk chair when George indicated that she should take it. She quickly pulled up the program and files that they needed, and proceeded to explain what Mrs. Hagerman didn't like about the designs, and what she wanted.

They were just finishing the first part of the layout, when a clear, high-pitched bell rang.

"What's that bell for?" Alex asked, looking up at George who was standing behind her.

"It's the dinner bell, scripture bell, or any bell Mom wants it to be to get our attention. This time it's for dinner. Mom doesn't like yelling for us. It's kind of like in *Sound of Music*, when Captain von Trapp uses the whistles with the children. She started using it after losing her voice calling us in one time when we were kids. Of course our friends tease us about it but they knew Mom well enough to not tease us much. Come on. She's the best cook in the area. Wins prizes for everything she enters into the fair."

After everyone was seated, Alex started to serve herself from the dish in front of her. She had just put a dollop of garlic mashed potatoes on her plate, when she realized that no one else was serving themselves. Instead they all had their arms folded and were bowing their heads, patiently waiting for her to do likewise.

Embarrassed, she quickly set the bowl down, held her hands in her lap and prepared herself for the prayer.

After the blessing on the food was over, Alex apologized. "Sorry about that. I'm used to having meals by myself, and I haven't said grace since I left home."

"No need to apologize, dear. We know not everyone is used to blessing their food. Now you just go ahead and serve yourself," Cherish told her.

During the meal the family talked about anything and everything. From politics to the wedding and birth announcements they had received that week to what Cherish's lesson was going to be the next Sunday. George noticed that Alex didn't say much, just ate her food, a wistful look on her face. Not wanting to draw everyone's attention to her, he directed a few questions or comments to her, but when she gave vague answers, he left her alone to her thoughts.

After dinner George and Alex went back to the office and continued to work.

"You were right, Cherish's cooking is wonderful. I haven't eaten that well in a long time," Alex said as she sat down, "Now, to the issues at hand. Mrs. Hagerman said she'd like some new winter outdoors pictures. She didn't like how these turned out for some reason. I'm not sure how we're going to do that, though, since we're over here. Do you have any ideas?" Alex asked.

"Yes. One of my college buddies, Max, manages a ski resort in Sun Valley that his family owns. I can give him a call and ask if we can come up this week and take some pictures. We can bring my family along and I can use them as the models. I'll just make sure I don't take any pictures of the lodge. I'll give him a call right now."

"Will we need a photographer?"

"No, I've been taking pictures for ages. Before I started the ad company with Pat, I seriously thought of doing photojournalism."

After making the call and getting permission to go over in the next day or two, George went to tell the family. In the living room, his mom, dad, and Jane were practicing the song they were going to sing at church for Christmas program.

"Hey guys, I have a favor to ask you. We need to go up to Sun Valley tomorrow or the next day to take some pictures. Would you be able to come and be the models? I'm going to call Doug and Nancy and see if they can come, too."

"I don't see why not. Your mother and I have been planning on visiting the Joneses before New Years, and this would be a good chance to do that. Jane, are you okay with going up?" Kurt asked.

"Sure. I've only been able to go skiing once so far this season. Will you let me take some pictures, too?"

"I don't see why not. If you get some good ones, we might use them."

"Great! Thanks George," Jane said as she went to give him a hug.

"I'd like to have a chance to tackle the slopes myself," Kurt said. "I'll stay on the small hill, dearheart," he said reassuringly, as he caught his wife's eye.

After determining that going in two days would work better for everyone, George went back to the office to call Doug and Nancy. Doug wasn't going to be able to make it, but Nancy said she'd love to go. After finishing the call, he turned back to the laptop to see what Alex had done while he was gone.

After another half hour, they had done all they could without new pictures.

The bell rang again.

"It's time for scriptures. Do you want to join us Alex? We're reading the New Testament. Every December we go through the first four books. We like to focus on the reason for the season as much as we can. You can read or not, as you like."

Alex declined, "No, that's okay. I think I'll go to bed now. It's been kind of a long day."

In the living room Cherish asked if Alex was going to join them.

"No, she said she wanted to turn in," he said.

As they read from Matthew, George tried to pay attention, but found it to be very difficult. He keep thinking of Alex as he saw her at the airport, of her in the jeep on the way to the house, and how she had turned prickly when she found out how much they loved Christmas. What could have happened that was so bad to make her not want to join in the fun? It was a question he was determined to get an answer to.

Chapter 2

The next morning Alex was already at the breakfast table when George walked in, wiping sleep from his eyes. He was barefooted, his hair was still tousled, and he was wearing green and red flannel pajama bottoms with a t-shirt that proclaimed 'If at first you don't succeed, try again' with a picture of someone climbing a cliff. In contrast, Alex sat at the table in a forest green chenille sweater shirt that looked like it had been custom made to fit her, and black jeans that hugged her like ivy on an old building. She wore just enough make-up to enhance her eyes and lips, and her hair was done in a French braid, a few tendrils escaping to caress her neck and cheek. For the second time in as many days, she took his breath away.

"Good morning, dear," his mother greeted him.

"Mornin'," he croaked, his throat tight from more than just waking up.

What was it about her that appealed to him? He'd seen and been with some very beautiful women before. He just didn't understand why without even trying she kept making it hard for him to breath.

"Would you like eggs or pancakes?" Cherish asked, as she handed him a glass of fresh orange juice.

After clearing his throat of the tightness that didn't seem to want to go away, he said, "I'll make myself a breakfast burrito. You probably haven't eaten yet, so you go ahead and fix yourself something."

"Thank you, dear," Cherish said, and she sat down at the table with a plate of pancakes she'd pulled out of the warming oven.

As he set about making his breakfast, George asked Alex how she'd slept.

"Quite well, I'm glad to say. It took me a while to go to sleep, but once I was out, I was out."

"Why did it take you so long to get to sleep?" he asked.

"I guess I'm not use to the quiet. I live in a studio apartment right next to a freeway. Even at two o'clock in the morning you can still hear enough traffic going by to let you know that you're not the only one that's awake. How close is your nearest neighbor, anyway? I don't remember seeing any houses since the last turn as we drove here," she said, then finished off the last of her blueberry pancakes.

"About a mile on the one side, a half mile on the other, and two miles on the back. We have about five acres of land and the rest belongs to the other families. All three are farmers," George told her.

"I've always lived in the city and I haven't traveled much to the country. I don't think Yellowstone counts. The one time I went there, it was during the peak season."

When George had finished making his burrito, he sat down next to Alex and said a silent prayer.

"Since we can't work on the brochure today, did you have any ideas as to what we're going to do?" Alex asked after he'd taken a swallow of juice.

"I hadn't made any plans, but since it snowed really well last night there's snowshoeing, horseback riding, shopping, all sorts of stuff to do."

"I haven't seen a barn. Do you have your own horses?"

"The barn is behind the house," Cherish answered. "We have three horses."

"What about you, George? Don't you have a horse for when you come home?"

"I did, but after college I wasn't able to come home very often, so we sold him. One of the guys I'd gone to high school with had married a lady with a five-year-old. As Thunder fortunately didn't live up to his name, they felt he'd be perfect for their son. It's seldom that we all are together and want to go riding, so I just borrow Dad's horse when I want to ride."

"I haven't been riding since the two summer camps I went to during high school. I'd like to go for a ride, if that's okay," Alex said.

Cherish had just finished eating and was taking her plate to the sink when she said, "It's perfectly fine, dear. It'll do George good. He hasn't had a chance to ride yet this trip. If you like, I can pack you a lunch."

"That would be great. Thanks Mom," George said, and went over to give her a hug and a peck on the cheek. Turning back to Alex he said, "It's only eight-thirty now. If we start saddling up the horses by eleven, it'll give us time to get to one of my favorite spots. Is that okay?"

"That'd be great. Only none of the shoes I brought are suitable."

"That's not a problem. We have a couple of extra pairs, just in case. What size do you need?" Cherish asked.

"I wear a size seven and a half."

"That's decided then," George said. "How about we go for a bit of snowshoeing first?"

"I've never been snowshoeing before. It sounds like fun."

After taking care of their dishes, George took a quick shower. Then they went into the garage to get the equipment that they would need, grabbing coats on their way. Once they had what they would need, they went out the back door and sat down on the porch steps to put on the snowshoes. When they were ready, they headed for the back of the property. With five acres the family had room for a nice barn and corral, a good-sized garden, raspberries and blueberries, and some fruit trees. As they walked, George told Alex what they were passing, whether or not it could be seen.

"Mom likes to keep busy in the summer, so she has a garden large enough to have everything that she'll need for the

21

next year. My favorite is the sweet corn and the peas. She freezes them so they'll taste as fresh as possible. The trees are a combination of apples, pears, apricots, peaches, and cherries. She cans as much as she can and either keeps it in our storage or gives it away to those in the area who may be going through hard times. The cherries are the best. Growing up, I would take a whole quart and eat it in one sitting. Man, they were good! I'll have to see if Mom has a jar and if you'd like, we can split it," he offered.

"That sounds wonderful. I don't know when the last time was that I had homegrown food. Cherries are my favorite, too.

"Snowshoeing isn't as hard as I thought it was going to be," she said after a while, panting slightly. "But it sure is showing me how out of shape I am."

"We can take a break if you like. I wouldn't mind one myself. I work out regularly, but I'm getting winded, too."

After another ten minutes they headed back to the house. When they got there, Jane met them in the garage. She asked them where they'd gone and if Alex had enjoyed snowshoeing.

"We were in the back yard. And yes, I did enjoy it," Alex said, smiling. Her cheeks were rosy and her eyes shining.

George caught a look in Jane's eye that he didn't quite trust. Almost like she knew something that he didn't. That had never worked to his favor growing up. He gave her a stern look which she returned with an innocent one of her own, the twinkle in her eyes letting him know she knew exactly what he was unhappy about.

"Did you want something, Jane?" he asked pointedly.

"Yes, I came out here for my snowshoes and noticed them missing. I figured that Alex was borrowing them, so when I saw you guys coming back, I came out here to meet you."

"Oh, I'm sorry," Alex said as she handed Jane the snowshoes in question.

"That's okay. They're there to be used," Jane said as she accepted the snowshoes. "What are your plans for the rest of the day?"

"We're going to go horseback riding and have a picnic around lunch time, then come back and figure out the rest of the day. I was going to ask you if Alex could use Starlight."

"Sure. She needs to be ridden," Jane said with a shrug.

After putting away the rest of their stuff, they went into the kitchen to see how lunch was coming. Cherish was mixing a big bowl of macaroni salad when they walked in.

"How did it go, dear?" she asked Alex.

"It was wonderful. You must have an amazing garden in the summer. George was telling me how you can all you can," she stopped, realizing how silly she sounded, and chuckled. "That's not how I meant that to come out."

"That's okay, dear. We joke about that every year. Speaking of canning, was there anything in particular that you wanted with lunch?"

"Yes. I was telling Alex about the cherries. Do you have a quart we could take with us?"

"Of course I do," Cherish said as she opened the pantry door. She quickly pulled out the desired jar and turned to him. "You should know I keep one up here, just for you, when you come for a visit."

"Aww, a mother who knows my heart," George said, clasping his hands over his chest. He then turned and winked at Alex, who was sitting at the table enjoying the exchange between mother and son.

"Why don't you go into the family room and play the piano while you wait? I haven't heard you play yet this trip," Cherish said as she went back to her preparations. "You won't mind, will you dear?" she asked Alex.

"I don't see why I would. I wouldn't mind taking a turn myself, if that's okay. I don't get to play as much as I'd like. Wouldn't want to get rusty."

"Come on, then. I'll play some of my favorite pieces for you."

When they got to the piano, George opened up the bench and sifted through the sheet music and pulled out his selections. After closing the bench, he sat down, set up the first song he wanted to play, ran though a couple warm-ups, then began to play a Russian ballad. The ballad was haunting, yet toe-tapping at the same time. Next he played an Irish jig that had Alex dancing in place. The last piece he played was an American folk song that he sang along with. It was a Romeo-Juliet story that ended with the two lovers running away from their families to start their own.

23

George's smooth bass floated through the room, wrapping the story around them. As the last notes died away, his hands remained poised over the keys as if they wanted to stay there forever, to play the last cord again and again so the song would never fade away.

"That was beautiful," Alex said very quietly, as if she, too, wanted to preserve the feel of the song in the room.

George let his hands fall onto his lap, a peaceful smile on his lips.

"I love that song. Have ever since I first played it. When I read the lyrics for the first time, I remember hoping that they would be able to be together, to teach their children to love others, despite their differences," he said softly.

Alex gently placed her hand on his shoulder. George covered her hand with his own and gently squeezed. After a minute he got up and indicated that she should play.

She went through the same process he had, going through the stacks of music in the bench, pulling out a few songs, sitting down, and warming up. While she did this, George sat down in a chair close to the piano where he could watch her profile. Alex started out with Für Elise, and then went into a sonata. Next she played another classical piece, this one from memory. George was mesmerized as he sat there watching her play, pouring her soul into the music. By the time she stopped, he had goose bumps on his arms and a warm feeling stealing into his heart.

When Alex turned to look at him, she had tears in her eyes that she did nothing to hide.

"I have always loved classical music. I think in part because my mother would play classical music records to help me get to sleep when I was young. Für Elise was one of her favorites. When she'd had a hard day, she would put it on and then she would dance to it."

"She knew ballet?"

"She must have known at least some. I'd watch her for as long as she'd dance. Then I'd try to mimic her in my room. One time she came into my room as I was dancing. She hugged me hard, and then showed me how to do the steps. After that, she let me dance with her."

By the time she finished speaking, the tears in her eyes were running unchecked down her cheeks, but there was a wistful smile on her lips.

"When we were little, mom had a small fish tank. On her hard days she'd sit in front of it and watch the fish swimming back and forth. She didn't have very many really bad days, but we knew it was a bad one if she was watching them at four in the afternoon," George said.

George got up, went over to Alex and helped her up. Then he gently wiped the tears off her cheeks. As he looked into her eyes, he saw shadows deep inside, ones that he knew he wanted to help her to chase away.

"Lunch is almost ready," Cherish called from the kitchen.

"We'd better, um, go get ready," Alex said as she looked away from George, breaking away from the gentle touch on her face.

George smiled gently at her back as she walked in front of him to the kitchen. He was happy to know he wasn't the only one thrown off track.

In the barn George walked over to a stall on the right and clicked his tongue to get the horse's attention. The chocolate brown horse turned her head and quickly came to see what treat was waiting for her. When her head came over the door, George petted the white blaze on her forehead as he crooned to her. Happy for the attention, she pushed into his hand and George chuckled.

"The horses we have left were born here. We used to have a herd of them, but now it's just the ones we need for the family. This lovey-duck is Starlight. She'll be yours to ride while you're here. She's Jane's horse. If you want to know the story behind the name, ask her. She loves to tell how she helped with the birth."

Starlight, having more important things in mind than just a scratch, started bumping George's shoulder with her nose and wuffling at his shirt pocket.

"What's she doing?" Alex asked.

"She thinks I have a sugar lump in my shirt pocket. I normally carry them there. But she's wrong. I have it in my pants pocket." And so saying, George pulled out the cube and let the horse have it.

25

Starlight rolled her eyes in ecstasy as the sweetness melted in her mouth. Alex laughed at the horse's look of utter contentment.

"I've never seen a horse so happy to get *one* lump of sugar, nor seen that human a look on an animal," Alex said, laughter in her voice.

Chuckling, George said, "She's always been that way. I think in part because we only give her sugar every so often. Normally it's carrots. Mom has a strict rule on how much and how often the horses are to get sugar."

After giving Starlight a piece of carrot as well and scratching behind her ear, he moved to the next stall. The horse there was waiting for his treat, his head already extended past the stall door.

"This lug is Charlie."

Alex gave a very unladylike snort of laughter.

"You get it then. Mom thought it would be nice to have a Charlie horse that didn't hurt--much. She got them all the time when she was pregnant with us. He's Dad's horse. Probably the most ridden horse we own right now. Dad prefers riding to driving around the ranch."

As he said this, he pulled out another lump of sugar and piece of carrot and fed them to Charlie. He then walked over to the stall to the left of Starlight's and petted the gray horse that had its head hanging over the stall door.

"This is Cinder, Mom's horse. Mom had been reading Cinderella to Jane when Cinder was born, and with her being a dappled gray, Jane thought it a fitting name."

Alex had come over to Cinder's stall and was scratching her behind the ear. Cinder, happy for the attention, was leaning into the scratching and all but smashing Alex's hand into the doorframe with the pressure she was applying to the hand scratching her.

"You'd better be careful with that," George said. "Cinder likes being scratched behind the ears so much that one time she almost walked me into the water trough to get me to scratch her as hard as she wanted. We'd better saddle up now and get this lunch on its way."

So saying, he headed over to the tack room, pulled down a saddle, and went to Starlight's stall. Alex opened the door, let George in first, then stepped in after him. After tossing a blanket over the horse's back, he threw the saddle on.

"I'll let you tighten the girth while I saddle up Charlie."

Once the horses were ready, George ran back into the house with two saddlebags. When he returned a few minutes later, he settled one saddlebag on each horse, and secured a blanket with a tarp bottom behind his saddle. Once they were mounted, he pulled two pairs of sunglasses, gloves, and ski caps out of his coat pockets, handed one set to Alex, and put the other set on.

As they rode, they talked about what books they'd read, what movies they'd seen, and what places they'd been, and discovered that they had a lot in common. The only other sounds they heard were occasional snorts from horses and the crunch from the horse's hooves in the snow.

They rode through the center of town, George waving to the few people who were out. When they reached the outskirts of the town proper, they followed a small stream, the water running under a thin layer of ice. They followed the stream for about a half-mile till it bent to the right. They crossed over it and headed left. After about another half-mile, they came to the base of a small hill that was liberally sprinkled with trees. They rode up the somewhat steep slope of the hill single file, between the trees.

"We're almost there," George said as the last set of trees came into view.

Behind him he could hear Alex's surprised gasp as they crested the hill.

A meadow completely surrounded by the trees lay before them, a blanket of white, untouched by anything but a few rabbits, birds, and deer. The snow, reflecting the winter sun, sparkled like millions and millions of tiny diamonds, almost blinding them despite the sunglasses.

"Up here I feel like I'm the only person on earth. Gives me a chance to be close to nature and myself," George said, as he dismounted, the snow only a couple of inches deep. He took off his sunglasses and put them back in his coat pocket. "Come on, let's tether the horses."

They loosened the girths and tethered the horses to a birch that stood further in than the rest of the trees. George then untied the blanket from the back of his saddle. The two of them spread it out, then unpacked the food. After they sat down, George blessed the food, then handed Alex a paper plate and plastic silverware. They helped themselves to the macaroni salad, cherries, ham sandwiches, and deviled eggs that Cherish had made for them. To drink they had a thermos of mint lemonade.

After eating for a bit, Alex looked up from her plate.

"This is the best macaroni salad I've ever had, and these cherries are just as good as you said. Most mac salad that I've had tasted off, but this is amazing."

"I'm glad you're enjoying it. I do feel that Mom's macaroni salad is the best. She's won two ribbons for it in the last three years at the county fair."

"And the lemonade. Where did Cherish learn to make it? It's the best I've ever had, better than my aunt's, and she made great lemonade."

"She learned at girl's camp one year when she was a leader. They were on a hike when they came across some wild mint. One of the other leaders knew how to make it and said they had some ingredients back at camp, so they picked some. Mom made sure she got the recipe and made it for us every year when we went camping or hiking."

They continued eating, commenting every now and then on whatever came to mind. After they were done, they put the remains of their meal away.

"Before you get too comfortable, there's something I want you to see," George said to Alex.

George helped Alex up, eager for her reaction, and they walked to the edge of the meadow near the place where they had come up.

"Oh, George," she said softly. "It's beautiful!"

With the leaves off most of the trees, they had an almost perfect view of the valley below. The snow covered most of the valley, making it look like a miniature village that one might find in a toy store.

"This is pretty much the only time you can see the town from here. If the trees have many leaves on them, they block the view," George said. Putting his left arm around Alex's shoulders, he stepped closer to her and pointed with his other hand. "Can you see the church steeple?"

"Yes."

"Look three fields back, just to the right. You see that house?"

"Yes. Is that your parent's?" she asked quietly.

George made a sound of agreement as he put his right hand down. They stood there, his arm still around her shoulders, for what felt to George like forever and no time at all. Then Alex stepped away from him, stepped up to a tree and leaned against it.

George felt her leaving like a piece of him had been ripped away. He longed to have her back in his arms, giving her the hug he sensed she needed, though he suspected she didn't know that she did. Not wanting to intrude on the silence he felt she needed, he turned, went back to the blanket, and lay down, tucking his hands behind his head, eyes closed against the brilliance of the sun. He lay like that for several minutes before he finally heard the crunch of her boots on the snow. She lay down next to him, her hands behind her head as well.

After a minute Alex asked, "Do you ever wonder why things happen the way they do? Whether you have control over what happens to you?"

Something in her tone of voice made George realize that his answer might mean a lot to her. Taking time to put his thoughts in order he replied, "Yes, and no. I know we have control over what we do. Most of the time we know, or at least strongly believe we know, what the consequences of those actions will be. So for that, yes, I do believe we have control over what happens to us. I also know that sometimes we make decisions that we don't know the consequences of.

"Do I wonder why things happen the way they do? Sometimes. Sometimes I can see why things turn out they way they do, usually after I'm out of the situation, but occasionally while I'm in it. The saying about hindsight being 20/20, well, I think it depends on how hard you look. Some people never learn, while others are always learning from what they've been through or from watching others.

"I know that we have a loving Heavenly Father who wants us to be happy, but, for better or worse, He's given us the opportunity to make whatever choices we will. That goes for how we react when we find out the consequences as well. I have seen and felt His guidance in my life, and I know that I haven't always listened to what He's tried to tell me. But I have always tried to learn from what happened. And when I go to Him, asking for forgiveness, while it hasn't always come right away, I have felt His love and forgiveness in the end. Does that answer your questions?"

"Mostly. I—Never mind," she said, shaking her head. "Can we go back now?"

The feeling of closeness they had shared was gone. Without saying a word, George got up and then helped Alex up. They readied the horses then mounted.

They were silent for most of the trip back, George speaking only to point out a rabbit at one time, a deer another. He wondered what had happened to Alex. She didn't like Christmas, and she was questioning what control one had over one's life. What had gone on in her past that had had such a negative effect on her and had been unresolved for this long?

About halfway home, George realized that if was going to help Alex overcome whatever it was she was giving hints about, it would be on her timetable.

He just prayed that he would know what to do or say to help her heal.

Chapter 3

"We're back, Mom," George called out as they stepped into the mudroom that was off the kitchen.

"Last time I checked, I was your dad. Did something happen and no one told me?" Kurt joked from the kitchen table, a game of checkers in front of him. "Did you both have a good time?"

"You know I always enjoy a good ride," George replied. "You'll have to ask Alex what she thought. She hasn't told me yet how she liked it."

"I enjoyed myself, thank you. It was nice to ride again after so many years. When I first got on Starlight, I thought I might not remember how to ride. After a few minutes, though, it all came back," she answered. "Including the fact that I'll need to take a hot bath tonight."

Kurt chuckled. "I know what you mean. Every now and then I still need one myself, especially since I'm getting old. These old bones don't ride as well as they used to."

"What are you talking about, 'old bones'? You just turned fifty a couple years ago," George said in mock disbelief.

Kurt looked at George, all joking aside. "I turned sixty this year, son, and when you've been riding as long as I have, what the horses haven't jarred loose, the arthritis gets. I didn't want to tell you yet, but since it's come up, I'm seriously thinking of hanging up my spurs, at least part of the time."

"But who would take over? Not Doug. He's never been into ranching, or farming for that matter."

George took a good look at his father, noting that the once raven hair was now mostly sliver. His skin had always been weathered, but it now seemed to have another quality about it that said his dad was getting on in years. The lines on his face were etched from years of laughing and hard work. The once broad shoulders that had made his dad look like Atlas when George was a kid were not quite as broad now, and his dad looked slightly stooped.

"Dad, is there something wrong?" George asked, concern for the man he'd looked up to all his life showing in his voice and on his face.

"With my health?" Kurt heaved a big sigh. "Yes, there is. Nothing major, mind, but something I need to pay attention to, nonetheless. I didn't want your mother worrying you with this before you got here. I had a mild heart attack about a week before you got here. The doc said I was okay, but to start takin' it easy. Start changin' my diet 'n all. Figured I'd start all that after the New Year."

"As to who would take over my responsibilities, our new foreman has been doin' really well. He has a boy about Jane's age that's been helpin' out, too. Between the two of them, I think we'll be fine."

"I really wish you'd let Mom tell me about your heart attack when it happened," said George, a note of hurt in his voice.

"There wasn't anything that you could have done to help and I didn't want you to get distracted. As you can see, I'm fine now. I plan on following Doc's orders so I'll be around for my grandkids."

The mention of grandkids reminded Kurt that they weren't alone. He turned to Alex with a smile of apology.

"I'm sorry, Alex. I forgot for a moment there that you were here. Didn't mean to air my problems in front of you. Cherish would have my hide if she found out."

"I'd have your hide if I found out what?" Cherish asked, coming into the room.

Kurt did something George had never before seen his dad do--he blushed to the roots of his hair. Never one to lie, especially to his wife, Kurt confessed.

"I forgot Alex was here and was tellin' George about my heart attack and about cuttin' back on the work."

"Normally I would have your hide, but since it means you finally told George what happened, I think I can let this one slide," Cherish said with loving sternness.

Cherish stepped over to Kurt, bent down, and placed a kiss on his forehead.

"If you don't mind, I think I'll take that hot bath now. My backside is reminding me that I haven't ridden in over five years," Alex said, reminding them of her presence.

"Of course, dear. You can use our tub. It's bigger and has water jets," Cherish told Alex. "George, why don't you finish this game of checkers with your father? I need to start dinner soon."

So saying, she led Alex to her bathroom.

George took the seat his mother had been using and looked at the game in front of him, trying to determine what move his mother might have had in mind next.

"Whose turn?" George asked.

"Yours. She doesn't say much, does she?" Kurt asked.

"Who, Alex? No, not yet. But what she does say says a lot. About what, I don't know yet," George said as he took his turn, jumping Kurt's piece. "King me."

Kurt set another piece on George's checker, then set about getting his own piece kinged.

"Sometimes it's not what's said, but what's *not* said that's more important. I know how hard it can be, wanting to help, not knowing if you should, or what to do. Have patience and faith. She'll open up when she's ready to. Knowing you, I should say that it shouldn't take too long. I've seen strangers open up to you when you were a teen, people who looked like they'd rather spit on you than accept your help. She'll come 'round."

33

"I know, Dad. I spent half the trip back coming to that conclusion. There's something in her past that has really hurt her. I don't know what yet, but I'm willing to wait. I know we're put where we can help."

Cherish came back shortly after that, turned on the CD player she kept in the kitchen, and started on dinner while the two men finished their game. The mood lightened when George tried to distract Kurt so he could move two checkers.

The game ended with Kurt stomping George's last two pieces in one move, and Kurt put the game away while George went to help Cherish with the apple pie. They were both singing along with the music, George's bass blending perfectly with Cherish's clear soprano, when Alex came back into the kitchen.

"Whatever you're cooking, it sure smells wonderful," she said as she leaned against the doorjamb. "I thought that with the lunch we ate I wouldn't be hungry so soon, but I guess I was wrong."

Her coppery hair was still damp from her bath, pulled back in a loose ponytail at the nape of her neck, and she hadn't reapplied her make-up. She was wearing a white V-necked sweater shirt with a pair of well-worn blue jeans and white flats.

Cherish jumped in surprise, almost dropping the pan of roast beef she was putting in the oven. Setting it down quickly, she placed her hand over her heart.

She turned quickly to face Alex. "Oh, dear! I haven't had a start like that in years. Didn't you learn not to sneak up on people while they're singing?" she said in her most affronted tone of voice. Then she smiled, letting Alex know she wasn't serious.

The family worked on preparing the meal for a bit then went to sit on the porch and enjoy the sun.

When dinner was about ready Cherish asked Alex, "Would you please come and help set the table? George always insists on setting it improperly."

"The fork *is* supposed to be on the right. I don't eat left-handed, and unless you are left-handed or in England, who cares?" George defended himself, winking at Alex to try to get her to play along.

She smiled back sweetly, then said, "Be that as it may, but I was brought up to make sure the table was set as if company were coming. We never knew if we'd have someone joining us at the last minute. My uncle was always inviting someone less fortunate home to join us. One time it was the mayor. He'd been having a bad day when my uncle bumped into him. Uncle said the best way to cheer up a bad day was to have a good meal, and he knew just where one was going to be served. Uncle comes home with the mayor in tow and Aunt almost had a fit. She'd cooked chicken that night and it hadn't turned out quite right. The mayor said it was the best chicken he'd had since he was a boy, and he meant it, so my aunt forgave my uncle. After that she'd brag about the mayor eating chicken at her table and repeat what he'd said. Let me tell you, I was never allowed to set the table improperly after that."

"See, dear. This young lady know exactly why it's important to set the table right," Cherish said. "Young lady, you stick around for a while and you might be able to fix what I've never been able to."

Throwing his hands up in defeat, George gave in. "All right, all right. I give up. The fork goes on the left. Sheesh, Alex, did you have to side with Mom? Now I'll never be able to get away with setting the table my way."

Behind Cherish's back, Alex did an impression of Groucho Marx waving an imaginary cigar and wiggling her eyebrows. George laughed, then turned to get the plates out of the cupboard.

Dinner was noisy as everyone talked to whoever would listen about what had happened that day. Alex joined in, seeming to be more relaxed after having gotten to know the family better. She laughed at Jane's story of her first college dance when someone had snuck the school mascot in, and the six-foot-long python named Monty had gotten onto the stage and scared the lead singer into falling into the drum kit. She asked Kurt questions about running a working ranch, and was fascinated to learn how much knowledge, skill, and luck it took to keep 200+ cattle where you wanted them. With Cherish she talked about cooking.

"I've never been much good in the kitchen. I always seem to mess up whatever I'm doing. I've found it's a lot easier to eat out, heat up frozen dinners, or open a can. I still mess up every once in a while, but I manage to keep myself alive."

"If you like, we can take an hour or so and I can show you something easy to make. I started out like you, without the microwave or take-out, but I learned and I know you can, too. You're a smart one, you just need a few pointers and some practice," Cherish offered.

"I'd like that," Alex said, smiling.

George watched Alex as the meal progressed. He was glad to see her open up and relax. She seemed to fit in very nicely with his family. She didn't let any teasing bother her --she gave it back just as good as she got--and she was getting to know everyone. The warmth in her eyes and smile was warming up the place that had emptied earlier when she'd pulled away from him in the meadow.

After dinner, Alex and George offered to clean up. While putting away the leftovers, George tried to find out more about Alex's childhood.

"You've mentioned your mom, aunt and uncle, but you haven't said anything about brothers or sisters. Are you an only child?" George asked, as he put a lid on the roast beef container.

"For all intents and purposes, yes," she said, looking down at her hands briefly. "I had a – a younger brother, but he died when I was seven."

"I'm sorry. I know how hard it can be to lose someone you love. How old was he?"

"Four. I don't like to talk about it," she said, opening the fridge door with more force than necessary.

"Okay, but if you ever change your mind, I'd like to hear about it. I have broad shoulders and my shirts are water-proof," he half joked.

Alex smiled slightly at his attempt to make her feel better. "Thanks. If I change my mind, I'm sure your shirts are going to be glad they're water-proof."

"What about pets? Did you ever have any?"

"Uh-huh. I've had a couple cats. My favorite one was Sara. My parents got her just before Mom found out she was pregnant with me. She almost made her thirteenth birthday before she died. Sara was always a comfort to me. She'd let me hold her when I was sad, never complained about how much I cried, or how red my eyes got. She'd just stay with me and purr."

36

"My favorite pet was the box turtle, Gulliver, that I had when I was about ten. Mom said I could have him if I took care of him, and it would absolutely be my responsibility to keep him alive. She firmly believed that if a pet was yours, it was yours in every sense of the word. She wouldn't do anything but buy the supplies and love it up. I'm glad she did it that way, though. It really helped to teach us kids responsibility, so that when we were allowed our own horses, we already knew that they came first."

They finished putting the food in the fridge and turned to wash the dishes.

"I always hated washing the dishes," George said. "How 'bout we flip for it?"

"Sure, it's not one of my favorite things to do, either."

George pulled out a quarter from his pocket. "Call it in the air."

"Tails," she replied, as the quarter almost hit the ceiling.

He slapped his hand over the coin, then peeked at it.

"A-ha! Heads. You wash."

Alex started filling the sink with water and soap while George leaned against the counter waiting for some dishes to rinse. They proceeded to wash and dry the dishes, content to be working in harmony. In the background Christmas songs could be heard as someone in the other room played the piano. After a few songs, the music stopped and Jane came into the kitchen.

"How's it going?" she asked as she headed over to the fridge.

"Fine. What are you looking for, you just ate," George scolded.

"You sound just like Mom. I'm looking for food, if you must know. I'm hungry again."

She pulled out an apple, rubbed it on her shirt, and took a bite. After she'd swallowed, she commented to Alex, "I see he roped you into washing. Please tell me he didn't flip a coin."

George sent Jane a warning glare, which she ignored.

"Yes, he did. Why?"

"You've been duped," Jane said, shaking her head. "He has a double-sided quarter he always uses. Took me a month before I figured it out."

Alex looked at George questioningly. George held up his hands and bowed his head, a grin belying his penitent stance.

"Guilty as charged," he said.

"Why, you!" Alex said, her hand skimming the soapy water, splashing it on his shirt.

George looked down at his shirt, unbelieving surprise on his face.

"I can't believe you just did that," he said. Looking up, a devilish grin spread across his mouth, a wayward blob of suds sliding down his chin. "Two can play that game, you know." So saying, he splashed her back.

In the two minutes it took Cherish to get to the kitchen to see what all the squealing and laughing was about, they managed to soak each other, the floor around them, and the counters behind them. George had the sprayer aimed at the top of Alex's head, while she tried to cover herself with her hands.

"What on earth has come over you, George?" Cherish demanded.

George immediately turned the water off and returned the sprayer, then stood looking as sheepish as he possibly could. Next to him Alex mimicked his pose, obviously embarrassed at being caught in a water fight in her hostess's house.

"She started it," George said quietly.

"I'm ashamed of you, George. Here you are, a--dare I say-- grown man, blaming a guest for something that I firmly believe you were at the bottom of. Besides, you know I don't care who started what. Now you clean up this mess. Alex, dear, you go change. Don't let George rope you into helping him." Cherish turned on her heel and left.

George and Alex stood there, completely embarrassed by the chastening. They looked at each other for a few seconds, then burst out laughing. Soon they were both laughing so hard that they sat down on the wet floor and leaned against the cupboards for support.

Meanwhile, Jane, who had escaped to the other side of the kitchen, just stood there watching them for a bit. She shook her head, and then left the room.

When they had themselves more or less under control, George stood up, held his hand out for Alex, and helped her up.

38

"We'd better do as Mother said. You don't want to find out what'll happen if we don't," he said, trying to control his breathing.

"I can't believe that just happened. I haven't done anything that irresponsible or impulsive in a very long time."

Chapter 4

By the time the kitchen was dry, George needed a hot shower. His damp shirt clung to his chest and his pants were all but dripping. He squelched his way to his room and grabbed a change of clothes before heading to the bathroom he shared with Jane. While he showered, he replayed what had happened. He was still surprised that he'd had a water fight. The last time he'd done that, he and Jane had been grounded for a week, plus they'd had to weed the garden every day for a month.

As he dried off and got dressed, he marveled at this new side of Alex. A man could have a lot of fun with a woman who wasn't afraid to get dirty, or wet, as the case may be.

He had just finished tidying the bathroom when the bell for scriptures rang. He went into the family room, found his scriptures, and sat down in his favorite chair. When the family had assembled themselves, Kurt asked Jane to say the opening prayer. After that, she started to read. As they took turns, George had to try very hard to concentrate on what was being said. When they were done, Kurt said the closing prayer.

After putting away his scriptures, George went to find Alex to make sure she knew what time they would be leaving the next day for Sun Valley. He knocked on her door but didn't get a response, so he checked around the house. Not finding her, he asked his mom if she had seen Alex.

"No, sorry. But I thought I heard the back door close a few minutes ago."

George walked to the back of the house, and through the window in the door caught a glimpse of the porch swing moving. He opened the door and stepped out. Looking over just enough to verify that she was there, he walked over to the railing that enclosed the porch. He leaned on the railing for a few minutes until Alex shifted in her seat.

"It's a beautiful night," she said. "I don't know how I'll adjust to going back to the noise of California. I know I work at the resort, but somehow, this is different. I don't stay the night there. I live an hour away in Placerville, next to the freeway. Placerville is big enough to make you forget that there's any nature around. And I've only lived there about seven months. Before that I grew up and went to college in Houston, with the exception of about six months in Vegas. I think that, outside of summer camp, this is the longest I've been away from a big city."

"It is beautiful. I always regret having to go back to the noise and smog. 'Marine layer', what a joke. To me there's nothing 'marine' about it. Smog is smog. The noise is the worst, though. I don't live right next to the freeway, like you, but I get enough honking horns and stuff to make me wish almost every day that I could move back here," he said.

Pulling himself upright, George turned to her. She had moved so that she was sitting sideways with her knees pulled to her chest, arms wrapped around her legs.

"As much as I'd love to stay out here with you, I need to get to bed. Sun Valley is about three hours from here and I'd like to get an early start. That's actually what I came out here for, to make sure you knew what time I'm planning on leaving. I'd like to be out of the house about nine. That way we can eat lunch when we get there, take the pictures, and still have some time to do some skiing before it gets dark. Will that be okay with you?"

"Not a problem. I'll be ready."

"Good. I'm going to bed now, then. I hope you sleep well," George said, pushing off from the rail and taking a step towards the door.

As he started to step into the house he paused, then turned back.

"Alex?" he said cautiously.

"Yes?"

"I…" Shaking his head, he changed his mind. "Don't stay out too long. Wouldn't want you to catch cold."

"I won't," she said softly, tipping her head on her knees so she could look out on the yard.

George paused another moment to just look at her before stepping into the warmth of the house. She looked so alone, almost lost, sitting out there in the cold. He realized that this might be the way she was used to living, outside the warmth of life, but he hoped she was ready to come in, because he was determined to help warm her heart. Living in the cold was no way to live. He'd seen firsthand what that could do to a person, and he didn't want to see that happen to her.

The next morning was a repeat of the day before. George walked into the kitchen still in his nightclothes, and Alex sat at the table looking like a million bucks in a green silk blouse, tight black pants, and black ankle boots, her hair in a French twist. This time he was wearing a T-shirt that had a picture of a kitten hanging from a rope. The caption read, 'Hang In There'. He was wearing the same flannel p.j.s he had the day before, again with bare feet.

"Orange juice," he croaked as he stepped into the kitchen.

Once again Cherish handed him a glass of fresh juice. After he'd taken a gulp he gave his mom a kiss on the cheek.

"Mom, you're the best. You almost always have my o.j. ready for me when I come in for breakfast."

"You're welcome, sweetheart. When are we supposed to leave for the ski resort?"

"In about an hour. Dad will be back from feeding the cattle, and I should be ready to go. Will that work of you?"

"That should be fine," Cherish said.

"I'll be ready to go as soon as I finish eating," Alex replied.

"Great. I'll let the others know."

After calling Nancy and letting Jane know, he sat down at the table. Cherish put a plate of eggs, hash browns, bacon, and sausage in front of him. After saying a quick blessing on the food, he dug in.

"Mmm-mmm. This is great, Mom. You've outdone yourself."

"As much as I love to hear that you enjoy my cooking, I have to bow out of this one. Alex cooked it for you."

George looked at Alex in surprise.

"But last night at dinner, you said you didn't know how to cook," he protested.

"Your mom offered me lessons. This was my first one. She told me exactly what to do, and I just did it. I'm glad you like it," she said, somewhat bashfully.

"If Mom wasn't here right now…" George let the rest of his sentence hang, looking at Alex in a way that left little doubt as to what he had in mind.

Alex held his gaze, but blushed furiously.

After a few seconds, George went back to eating his breakfast, a satisfied smile on his face. Alex finished her breakfast, took her dishes to the sink, and then left the room, all without looking at George. Cherish bustled around the kitchen for a few minutes before leaving.

George took his time finishing his breakfast, savoring the flavors and basking in the knowledge that Alex had cooked it for him. She was a wonder. Every time he turned around, she did something new to surprise him. Not that he wanted her to be predictable; he was just amazed at how much he had to learn about her. He hoped he never stopped learning.

After he'd taken care of his dishes, he went to his room and grabbed some clothes suitable for the ski resort. He then went into the bathroom to shave and brush his teeth. Once he was ready for the day, he went to find Jane and let her know they were about ready to leave. He found her in Starlight's stall, brushing her down.

"Hey, Squirt. We're going to be leaving in about half an hour. You going to be ready?"

"You bet. I'm almost done here, then I'm going to get ready," she said. "I think you should marry her."

"What? Marry? Where did that come from? I've only just met Alex and you already have me married to her?" George asked in surprise. He thought he'd been keeping his feelings pretty well under wraps.

"I've seen the way you look at her. When anyone's watching you're as normal as can be, but as soon as you think no one's looking, you get this look in your eyes like Dad gets when Mom's done something really special for him. She's okay, too. I'd like another big sis to help even the playing field some more. Don't get me wrong--I love Nancy, but she doesn't seem to have the same spunk that Alex does."

"I know what you mean about spunk. Okay, tell you what. You don't mention me marrying her to anyone else, and I'll think about it. Deal?" he asked, holding out his hand.

Jane tipped her head to one side and squinted at him while she made up her mind. Finally she straightened and shook his hand.

"Deal. On one condition."

"What's that," he asked cautiously.

"You don't wait too long to make up your mind. I don't think she's the kind to stick around long if she doesn't have a reason to."

"I'll see what I can do. Now hurry up. You're covered in horse hair and I don't think you'll look as nice for the pictures that way."

Laughing when she playfully stuck her tongue out at him, he left to get his equipment together.

Back in the house, he went to the darkroom that his parents had been kind enough to set up for him when he was in high school. He got out a small black shoulder bag and packed it with several rolls of film, a light meter, a notebook and pen, and his favorite camera. In another bag he put a good quality digital camera and extra lenses. He wanted to make sure that he'd get all the pictures he needed on this one trip. After making sure he had everything he needed, he went to find the rest of the family.

In the living room he found everyone waiting, except his dad.

"Is Dad coming?" he asked Cherish.

"Yes, he'll be here in a second. He just needed to make sure we have the Jones' address. We're supposed to meet them for an early dinner."

When Kurt joined them, they all headed for the garage. Since Kurt and Cherish were to visit their friends afterwards, they drove themselves while the other four piled into George's jeep.

"When we get up there, we'll make sure you have some snow boots. Wouldn't want you to freeze or anything," George told Alex.

"Thanks. I wasn't quite sure what I was going to do. I really didn't pack for extracurricular activities, and I wasn't sure if they would have anything up there. To tell you the truth, I've never been skiing before."

"I'll have to see about fixing that. I'm not great at it, but I do enjoy a good run down a decent slope," George said.

On the three-hour-long trip, Alex got to know Nancy. Nancy told the story of how she'd met Doug, and about some of the troubles they'd had before tying the knot. Alex laughed and commiserated with her over the troubles of love. Even though George and Jane had heard the story before, they also joined in, ribbing Nancy for not giving Doug the comeuppance he deserved for being so slow to see what a good thing he had. By the time they reached the resort, Alex and Nancy were well on their way to becoming friends.

After parking, George's group met up with Kurt and Cherish and went into the lobby of the hotel that was connected with the ski resort. George went to ask about Max while everyone else sat down in the waiting area.

"George, old buddy! How you doin'?" Max said, coming over to pump George's hand and slap him on the shoulder, careful not to hit the camera bag that was hanging over his shoulder. "It's been too long since I saw you last."

"I'm great, Max. You never look any different than you did when we were in college," he said, taking in Max's dark good looks.

"I think young, therefore I am young," Max said, smiling. "But come, let me say hi to your folks before I go back to taking care of all the problems that'll find my desk in the next five minutes."

George and Max walked over to where George's family was waiting, and George knew the exact moment when Max realized that Alex was with them. In college, Max tried to steal away every girl that he set his sights on, regardless of whether she was George's or any other guy's. George should have remembered this, but hadn't.

Max, all properness, made sure he greeted everyone else before turning his attention to Alex.

"Kurt, how are you? Still riding hard?" Max said, shaking the other man's hand.

"I am for the moment, but it looks like I'll be takin' it easy soon."

"That's too bad," Max said, concern in his voice. "Nothing serious, I hope."

"Not if I slow down and make a few changes."

"Well, I'm glad you're okay. Wouldn't want you kicking the bucket any time soon, would we?" Max said.

Turning to Cherish, he gave her a hug of real affection and kissed her cheek.

"And how are you, Mom?"

"I'm doing very well, dear. How have you been? You look like you're not eating enough," she said, looking at him critically.

"Always the mother hen," Max said, smiling as he shook his head. "I'm fine. I eat all my greens, like a good boy."

"Yes, but are they the right greens? I know you. You'll eat anything green as long as it's not a vegetable."

"You wound me!"

"But tell me I'm wrong," Cherish said with a smile.

"No, you're right, as usual," Max conceded.

Next Max turned to Nancy, whom he'd only met once or twice, but had gotten along with very well.

"I don't need to ask how you're doing, Nancy. You're positively glowing! Doug's treating you right? You know that I'll take you in a heartbeat if he's not," he said jokingly.

"He still treats me like a princess, just as he should," she said, smiling. "He said to send his regrets, but the office has him chained to his desk at the moment."

"Tell him we'll have to get together soon, and he's buying to make up for not being here today."

46

"Will do."

"Jane! I hardly recognize you. You've grown another couple of inches since I saw you last, and there's something's different, isn't there?"

"Hi Max," she said, giving him a hug. Pulling back, she bared her teeth.

"That's it! No braces! So now that you're all grown up and beautiful, are you dating up a storm?"

Jane blushed slightly at the compliments. "No, but I do have a couple of guys that I'm seeing somewhat regularly."

"Good for you. Don't limit yourself until you're ready to," Max advised, giving her a wink.

"And who is this gorgeous creature, George?" he said, finally turning his attention to Alex. "Don't tell me she's your girlfriend. She's way outta your league. Max A. Million at your service," he said, bowing in courtly fashion over her hand and kissing it gently.

"Is that your real name?" Alex asked as she gently retracted her hand from his hold.

"No, it's just what he thinks he's worth," George answered for his friend. "His name is Mumm."

"No, it's because I'm one in a million," Max retorted.

"Well, Mr. Mumm, how do you know George isn't the one out of my league?" Alex asked, seeming to be amused by Max's flirting. "And for the day, I just might be his girlfriend."

Max looked at her in disbelief for a second, then shook his head. "No. You're defiantly out of his league."

"If a man's lucky, he marries above him," Kurt put in.

"Probably," Max consented. "Well, I need to get going. The guys in the equipment rental know that you're here, so you shouldn't have any problems getting your gear, and it's on the house. If you're not done with it when you go to lunch, just ask them to hold it for you. Feel free to have full rein of the resort while you're here. If you like, I'll meet you in the restaurant at, say, 1:30? I'll treat you all to lunch."

George thanked Max for his help, and agreed that that was a good time.

George led everyone to rental shack. After everyone had skis and boots, they went outside and waited for George to find the first place to take some pictures. After a few preliminary shots, he decided to take pictures of them on the slopes.

"Alex, I'm sorry to do this to you, but since you don't ski, would you wait for us down here? You can either go over to the bunny hill to get some practice, or you can wander around for a bit. I don't want to risk your coming with us without knowing what to do. We should be back in about half an hour, forty-five minutes tops, if that's ok? I'll make it up to you later," George said apologetically.

"That's perfectly fine with me. I don't feel like killing myself on anything more dangerous than the bunny hill right now, anyway. Don't worry about me. I'll meet you at the bottom by the lift."

"If you don't mind, dear, I think I'll bow out of this one, myself," Cherish said. "You know I'm not very fond of skiing. I'll keep Alex company while you guys enjoy yourselves."

"Sure, Mom. We'll see you soon."

The two ladies were left standing there as the others went to the ski lift and waited for their turn to get on. When it came, George got on with Kurt, while Jane and Nancy rode together. Once at the top, they all gathered to one side to hear what George had in mind.

"I'll go down first and find a spot to take pictures of you guys as you ski down. Once you've passed me, stop at the side and we'll do it again. That way I should be able to get you at several different angles, by yourselves and in groups. Dad, you go first, then Jane, and then Nancy. Wait about five minutes before you start, Dad, then you two pace yourselves about two minutes behind one another. Everyone understand?"

They nodded, and George started down the slope. When he was about a third of the way down, he slid to a stop near the right side, and stepped out of his skies. He turned around and pulled out his digital camera, making sure it was set properly. After getting himself into the position he wanted to use, he waited for Kurt to start his descent. As soon as George could see Kurt, he started snapping pictures, following Kurt's progress till he was a few yards past where he was standing.

"That's good!" he called out, and watched as Kurt slid to a stop out of the way of the other skiers.

George turned back quickly as Jane, then Nancy, came rushing down. He repeated the procedure with each of the women. After Nancy had pulled to the side and stopped, George put the camera back into its case, snapped on his skis, and pushed off. When he was almost level with the others he, too, pulled over to the side.

Once he was close enough, he explained how he wanted the next shots. He then skied about another third of the way down, pulled over, stopped, and waved. This time Nancy and Kurt skied close together, Nancy just behind and to the right of Kurt. After they had passed George, they pulled over to wait for Jane and George. George watched for Jane and snapped a few more pictures before she pulled to the side where the other two waited for her. Once George had joined them, he told them that for the next pictures, he wanted them to ski down all together, with Jane, who was the best skier of the bunch, doing a jump, if she could.

When he got to the bottom of the slope, George turned and waited one last time. The three came down, spaced just as he'd hoped they'd be. Jane was even able to make a good jump.

"That was fun!" Jane said as she slid to a stop just in front of the others. "They have a good powder today. I can't wait for a chance to do a full run or two."

"You'll get your chance," George promised. "Right now we need to go meet the women folk and see about a few more shots before lunch."

They skied side by side to the ski lift and found the two women waiting for them.

"Have you been waiting long, honey?" Kurt asked Cherish.

"No, we got here just in time to see Jane make that jump," she said.

"My heart jumped to my throat when I realized that it was Jane," Alex said. "For some reason I wasn't sure if you were going to land properly or not."

"Na. I've been skiing for so long that something would really have to go wrong for me to mess up such an easy jump," Jane said.

"Enough chit-chat. I need to take a few more shots before we're supposed to meet Max. I saw a spot as we came over here that I think will work well."

They followed George to the spot he indicated and waited for his instructions. For this one, he wanted them to just walk around carrying their skis and poles. After a dozen or so pictures with the regular camera, George called it quits. They took their equipment back to the rental. Kurt and Cherish decided to turn theirs in as they were going to leave after lunch to go Christmas shopping before meeting the Jones'. Everyone else asked to have their skis held for them.

When they got to the restaurant, George asked about Max.

"Mr. Mumm isn't here yet, but he said he'd only be a few minutes. We'll seat you and you can go ahead and order," said the maitre d'.

After being seated, they ordered their drinks, and then looked at the menu. They were in the middle of ordering their food when Max stepped up to the table.

"I'm sorry I'm late. I had to take a phone call," he said as he sat down.

Once they had all ordered and the waiter had left, Max wanted to get caught up on the family news. He'd been a regular at the Hart residence during college breaks since his family had moved to England during his freshman year.

They spent most of the meal going over what had happened to each of them in the last couple of years, then did some reminiscing. Max flirted with Alex the entire time. When Max found some reason to touch Alex for the third time in as many minutes, George started to get annoyed. He knew that he didn't have any right to be jealous, but good grief! Couldn't the man keep his paws to himself? They weren't in college any more. Did Max still have to have every girl at his beck and call? George sent warning glares Max's way, but Max either didn't notice them, or was purposely ignoring them. Alex, in the meantime, seemed to be enjoying Max's attentions.

At one point Max glanced over at George with a look in his eye that seem to say, "See, I've still got it, and I've got you're girl."

George was so worked up that it took him a while to realize that his mother was talking to him.

"What? I'm sorry. What did you say?" he asked her.

"I asked if something's wrong. You've hardly touched your steak, dear."

"Uh, no. No, I'm fine. Just something of a headache."

He couldn't believe it. He'd just lied to his mother. He hadn't done that since he was in grade school and his first grade teacher had sent him home for picking a fight with another boy over whose father was the better rancher. He'd never picked a fight again, either.

"If you're sure, dear. I think I have something in my purse," she said, picking up her purse to look for something for him. Something in her voice made him think that she knew what was really wrong.

Having lied, he didn't feel like embarrassing himself further by not taking the offered medicine, so he swallowed the pills with a drink of water. After that he tried to hide his inner torment better.

The meal was almost over when the waiter came over and told Max there was a problem that he needed to resolve at the front desk.

"I'm sorry, guys. The boss's job is never done," he said as he got up. "I hope you'll stay and get some skiing in; this is the best powder we've had this season. Have a good day, and I hope to see you again before you go back to California, George, Alex."

"I hope so, too," Alex said sincerely.

"Sure," George said as casually as he could. He couldn't remember a time since that last fight in first grade when he wanted to punch someone's lights out as badly as he did Max's.

Finally and reluctantly, Max left. Some of George's anger left with him.

George applied himself to his lunch, and by the time everyone was finished, he had himself under better control. Why should it bother him if Max flirted with Alex? Alex was a beautiful and funny young woman. Besides, she was going home with him, not Max. And the chances of the Max and Alex getting together before she went home? Well, George didn't think they were too high. With any luck they'd have the layouts finished in the next day or so, and then Alex would be leaving.

The empty and almost panicky feeling that accompanied that thought was almost more that George thought he could bear.

He looked at Alex and came to a decision--one he would implement once they were home.

After lunch, Kurt and Cherish took their leave, and the others went outside to see what George had in mind for the remaining pictures. After looking around for a bit, he decided to take pictures of the others just goofing around. All three women were up for that. Jane immediately scooped up some snow and packed it into a snowball, which she threw at Alex. It hit her square in the chest. Fortunately Alex had zipped up her coat when she'd come outside. Alex was game, so before Jane could throw a second snowball, Alex had made one of her own and launched it at Jane.

Before either of them could make another snowball, they were both hit. They turned to see Nancy, who was getting more snow ready. Alex and Jane looked at one other, then at Nancy, and both grabbed up some snow. In seconds there was a free-for-all with George taking pictures like crazy, ducking every once in a while to avoid being hit. After he'd finished a second roll of film, he whistled sharply. All three women stopped what they were doing and looked at him.

"Okay, that's enough. I think I have what I need," he said, as he put the camera back in its bag.

He was just zipping the bag up when he felt a snowball hit him on his neck. Cold, wet snow made its way inside the collar of his coat. He slowly wiped it away before looking at the three of them. Nancy and Jane immediately pointed at Alex, who was standing between them. Carefully setting his bags down, he advanced towards the culprit.

"Jane, get my bags and guard them with your life."

Paying no more attention to Jane or his camera bags, he continued his slow advancing. Alex stood her ground, another ball of snow already being shaped in her gloved hands. Just when she was about to throw the ball, George pounced on her, scooping her up. Startled, Alex dropped the snow and clung to his neck.

"George! No, George!" she said, struggling once she realized where he was taking her.

Next to some trees a couple yards away was some fresh unpacked snow, piled high by a snowplow earlier.

"Oh, yes. I think you need to understand what it's like to have snow down your neck. Then maybe you'll think twice about doing that again."

He crossed the last few feet quickly, with Alex still fighting to be set free. George didn't even bother to try to disentangle her from his neck. He fell forward, Alex still in his arms, right into the middle of the biggest pile of snow. Once his mission had been accomplished, he quickly got up. He stood there and laughed at the expression on Alex's face as the snow went down her collar and started to seep into her pants.

The next thing he knew, he was on his own back, with snow sliding down his collar again. She'd hooked his leg, pulling him off balance and into the pile of snow beside her. She scrambled to her feet, trying to swipe the snow away from her clothes and neck.

"Serves you right," she gloated. "Next time you dump me in a pile of snow, I may not be so nice."

He hooked his foot around her leg, pulling her down on top of him.

"Maybe *I* won't be so nice, next time," he warned in return. He rolled them so that they were lying next to each other, his arms loosely around her. As they looked into each other's eyes, the laughter draining away as a more powerful feeling began to seep into them.

"I got some great shots!" Jane called as she hurried over to them, careful to stay far enough away that they couldn't pull her down, too.

George muttered something under his breath about pesky sisters who didn't know when to keep their mouths shut, and got up, offering a hand to Alex to help her up. Standing, they helped each other brush the snow off their clothes.

"Come on guys, let's go inside and get warmed up before we leave," said Nancy. "I'm starting to freeze out here."

Jane and Nancy turned and walked in front of them. With their attention elsewhere, George took off his glove and reached out for Alex's hand. She pulled her hand away, quickly took off her own glove, and took his hand again. They looked at each other for a second, smiled, and started walking.

When they reached the main walk area, George asked if anyone was up for hot chocolate or cider. They all were, so they headed back into the restaurant. Once they were seated and had ordered, Jane told George about the pictures she'd taken. He affirmed that there should be enough shots to use for the layout.

After they'd finished their drinks, George told them that if they wanted to get some skiing in, they'd better get going. Jane and Nancy went to get their skis and poles.

"Did you get a chance to practice on the bunny hill when you were with Mom?" George asked Alex.

"No, your mom and I mostly just talked while we watched the skiers."

"I'm sure you did, about me, right?" he asked dryly.

"Some. Did you really have Power Ranger pjs when you were twelve?" she said, trying hard to suppress her laughter.

"So what if I did? I thought they were cool," he defended.

Alex laughed. "Don't worry. I had a Barney toy at that age. But if you tell anyone, I'll deny it."

Changing the subject he asked, "Would you like to have a ski lesson? Or would you rather stay inside where it's warm?"

"I think I've had enough snow for one day. I noticed a couple of stores off the lobby. Maybe we could go in there and see what they have."

"Sure. Let's go tell the other two where we'll be," he said, as he picked up the camera bags.

They found Jane and Nancy just getting in line for the ski lift.

After telling them where he and Alex would be, Jane said, "We're going to go up to the second run."

"Have fun and be safe, you two," he said.

"Yes, Mother," replied Jane with loving sarcasm.

Chapter 5

Once inside the first gift shop, they made a circuit of the store, stopping every now and then to take a closer look at something. They came to a display case with glass figurines. Alex picked up one that was a music box and wound it up. Für Elise played as the couple on top circled each other in a dance.

"I love glass figurines," she said. "They're so pretty and delicate."

She put the music box down and gently touched a figurine of a humming bird on a morning glory vine.

"Do you have any?" George asked.

"No. I don't have a place at home to display them. A studio apartment gets crowded very fast, and mine's pretty full as it is."

Alex saw a little toy skier and decided to get it. When they got to the register, George pulled out his wallet to pay for it.

"No, I'll get it," Alex said.

"Let me," George insisted. "After all, I promised to make it up to you for making you wait while we were on the slope."

Alex finally gave in and let him buy the toy for her.

They were just about to leave to check out another store when Nancy and Jane came in, looking happy and sun-kissed.

"How was your run?" Alex asked.

"It was great! I did some of my best jumps. I did knock into this guy, though. He said it was his first time skiing down anything more challenging than the beginner's run. He apologized and asked me for my number," Jane said, all but jumping up and down in her excitement.

"He was very sweet about it. He even offered to take her skiing again to make up for it," Nancy added, smiling at Jane's enthusiasm.

Alex agreed that it was very nice of the young man, and then asked where the ladies' room was. Nancy said she needed to go, too, so the two left, following George's directions.

Once they were gone, George asked Jane for a favor.

"I want to get something for Alex, but I don't want her to know. Would you carry it for me until we get home?"

"Sure. What are you getting her?"

"Promise you won't tell anyone, not even Mom."

Jane gave a long-suffering sigh. "I promise."

George took her over to the glass figurines and picked up the music box and the hummingbird.

"Wow, those are really nice," Jane said. "I think she'll really like them."

"I know she will. Let's go pay for these before they get back."

After he paid and the figurines were boxed up, Jane took them. Shortly after that Nancy and Alex came back.

Noticing the bag in Jane's hand, Nancy asked what she'd bought.

"Just a couple of presents," she evaded smoothly.

"What did you get?" Alex asked.

"I'd rather not say. I want it to be a complete surprise."

George then asked if everyone was ready to go. They all decided that they were, so they left.

Once they were out of the mountains, George asked if anyone wanted to do any shopping on the way back.

"Sure. I haven't had a chance to start looking for Doug's gift yet. Do you mind if we stop at the mall on the way back?" Nancy asked.

"No, that's fine with me," said George. "Anyone object?"

As neither Alex nor Jane objected, George drove to the mall. Once they arrived, Alex said she was rather tired and preferred to sit and wait for the others. George said he'd wait with her since he had his shopping done. They agreed to meet by the food court in an hour. While Jane and Nancy walked to the mall map and tried to decide where to go, George and Alex wandered in the direction of the food court.

They walked in comfortable silence, stopping to window shop if something caught their eye. Once they got to the food court, they found a seat where they could people watch.

"Have you ever played the game where you make up stories about the people you're watching?" George asked.

"No. What kind of stories?"

"Anything that strikes your fancy. Take that man over there," he said, pointing to a harried-looking man in a three-piece suit. "I'll bet he's in such a hurry because he just found out that his in-laws will be spending the holidays with his family – an extended visit. He wasn't expecting to see them at all this year, so he hadn't thought of getting them anything other than a fruit basket or one of those fancy salami and cheese baskets. He knows that his father-in-law is very hard to please, so now he's starting to look for something he won't be criticized for. Now his mother-in-law is a bit easier to shop for. The more expensive it is, the better she likes it. So for her, he has to find something that costs enough, but won't make him miss his mortgage payment next month."

Alex wholeheartedly joined in making up stories. As they made up story after story, each became more preposterous than the last.

"Stop, stop," Alex said, gasping for breath. "I can't take it any more!"

Wiping tears out of his own eyes, he agreed, "Okay, I'll stop. I don't know if I could think of a better story than that last one, anyway."

They were still trying to calm down when Nancy and Jane found them.

"He's been doing the people-watching stories, hasn't he?" Jane asked, setting her bags next to her chair.

"You know me too well," he said.

"The first, last, and only time he did that to me," Nancy said, setting down her own bags, "I just about wet my pants. Fortunately for me, we were right next to the restrooms. I've never let him tell those stories again for fear that the next time I won't be so lucky."

"I'm hungry," announced Jane.

This prompted a discussion as to where they should eat. Since they couldn't agree on a place, they went their separate ways, and then met back at the table. George opted for Chinese, Nancy for a sandwich, Alex for pizza, and Jane had decided on Italian.

After sitting down, George, Nancy, and Jane automatically bowed their heads for a moment, silently blessing their food. Alex belatedly followed their example. Prayers over, everyone tucked in. They ate in silence, enjoying one another's company. After they finished and dumped their trash, they decided it was time to go home.

Once in the jeep, George turned on the CD player. They were instantly surrounded by the mellow sounds of Kenny G playing Christmas songs. The trip home was quiet. The combination of the music and the day's excitement finally took its toll on everyone. By the time they pulled up to the house two hours later, all three women were asleep.

George chuckled to himself as he quickly and quietly unpacked the jeep. Leaving the door into the house open, he went to Alex's door and carefully unbuckled her seat belt. Sliding his hands under her knees and behind her neck, he picked her up. She stirred, and he waited until she settled back down. He carried her to her room and gently laid her down on the coverlet.

She's so beautiful, fragile yet strong, he thought. *I wonder if I really stand a chance?* After a moment he left Alex to go and wake Jane and Nancy.

Once she was awake, Nancy decided to go home while Jane and George decided to wrap the presents they'd bought that day.

Afterwards, George held the wrapped boxes in his hands, wondering if he'd be able to give them to Alex on Christmas, or if he'd have to give them to her as she prepared to board her flight. He wanted very much to be able to watch her open them, to see surprise and joy fill her face. He set the boxes on his dresser and followed through with the decision he'd made at the ski resort. He knelt down beside his bed and poured out his heart to his Heavenly Father.

He prayed that he would continue to have patience with Alex; that she would open up to him at some point. Then he prayed that he would know if he should ask her to marry him. He knew that he was really close to loving her with his whole heart. Before he got there, he wanted to have an idea of whether they could have a future together. The best way to do that, he knew, was to ask the one person who truly knew everything. Things might not go the way he the way he hoped they would since everyone had their agency, but he'd have a better idea of what the Lord had in mind for him. After closing his prayer, he stayed where he was, trying to feel what he should do.

A few minutes later he got up and went to get his cameras. He took the two bags into the darkroom and began to develop the pictures he'd taken earlier. He felt himself go into a sort of trance as the familiar process soothed his mind. He was therefore surprised when he heard a knock on the outer door.

"Who is it?" he called out.

"Alex. May I come in?"

"If you wait about five minutes, you can."

"Okay."

Five minutes later he called out to her that she could come in.

"Make sure you close the first door before opening the second one," he said, as he heard the first door open.

"Why are there two doors?" she asked once she was inside.

"To keep the light out while the film is developing. After that, I can turn on the red light. That way I can see and it doesn't ruin the film," he explained. "If you'll just stand over here. It's not a large room and I need to be able to move about. Did Jane tell you where I might be?"

59

"Yes. She said that you almost always 'hole up' in here after taking pictures."

For the next while George went about the process of developing the pictures. Alex stood where he had directed her and asked questions every once in a while. Once the first roll was done, George hung the film up to dry. Then the two of them left the darkroom and went to the office to look at the pictures taken with the digital camera.

"I know I got some really good shots," George said, as he sat down at the desk and connected the camera to the computer.

As they looked through the pictures, Alex commented on how well the action shots had turned out.

"Some of my favorite types of pictures are action shots. To try and capture the energy and motion on a still frame is a challenge that I love to face."

They were able to pick out a couple pictures that worked well for the layout.

"I'll finish developing the second roll tomorrow, then make enlargements. We can look at them tomorrow night, or the next morning, depending on how many pictures I think we can use. We're not in that much of a hurry to get this done. Is there anything else in the layout you want to look at?"

"No, I think we've about covered everything we can without the rest of the pictures. Do you think we can use any of them?" Alex asked.

"I'm pretty sure there are at least one or two, and who knows what Jane took.

"It's not late yet, would you like to watch a movie, play a game, or something?" George asked, changing the subject.

"Let's take a look at the movies first," she said.

They left the camera on the desk and went into the family room. George showed her where the movies were kept, and she looked through them.

"How about *Princess Bride*?" she asked.

"Sure. Have you seen it before?"

"No, but I've read the book."

"I'll try very hard to not quote lines, then. Would you like some popcorn, or something to drink?"

"Popcorn and a soda would be great."

They went into the kitchen, made up a big batch of popcorn, and poured warm caramel topping all over it. Alex carried the bowl of popcorn while George brought two cans of soda. They set their food on the coffee table and George put the movie into the player. Alex took off her shoes, sat down, and tucked her feet up next to her. Before sitting down, George ran back to the kitchen for napkins. When he got back, he sat down and picked up the popcorn, and carefully picked out a couple of gooey pieces as the movie started.

By the time the movie was over, the popcorn was gone and they had had two cans of soda each.

"That was a great movie. I think they did an amazing job of adapting the book for a movie," Alex said, then got up and stretched.

"We've seen it so many times that we can practically quote the whole movie," said George.

He picked up the empty bowl with the soda cans in it, and took it into the kitchen. Just as he was throwing the cans into a recycle bin, the phone rang and he answered it.

"Hart residence, George speaking,"

"Hey, George. It's Jane."

"Where are you? I thought you were home."

"I decided to go riding, and I've had a bit of trouble. Starlight caught her hoof on something while I was riding and I had to walk her to the nearest home. I just got to a phone. Are Mom and Dad home yet?"

"No, but I'll hook up the trailer to the jeep and come get you. Where are you?"

After getting directions and a phone number to use if he needed to call her, he hung up the phone.

"Was that Jane?" Alex asked.

"Yes, I'm going to have to go get her. Want to come?"

"No, I think I'll stay here."

"Okay, but here's my cell number in case you need anything. I should be gone about twenty to thirty minutes."

George grabbed his coat and a heavy-duty flashlight, then went to hook up the horse trailer to his jeep.

When he found the address that Jane had given him, he parked the car and went to the door. Shortly after he knocked, Jane answered the door. She launched herself into his arms and gave him a big hug.

"You're the best, Gorgy-Porgy. Thanks for coming to get me."

A woman came up behind Jane. When Jane realized she was there, she made introductions.

"George, this is Carol; Carol, my brother George. I want to thank you for letting me use your phone and stay here while I waited for him."

"No problem. Feel free to visit any time," Carol said. "Would you like to come in for a moment, George?"

"I'd like to, but we'd better be going. I'd like to get Starlight home as soon as I can."

"Of course. How silly of me. I'll go with you to get her."

Carol led the way to the horse, which was tied to the rail of the back porch. George untied the reins and led everyone back to the jeep.

"I'd like to take a look at her leg before we put her in the trailer," he said. "Jane, will you get the flashlight out of the front seat?"

Jane brought the flashlight back, turning it on and holding it for him. George felt up and down the leg he'd seen Starlight favor, and noted a little bit of swelling.

"I think she'll be fine. We just need to let her rest that leg for a few days. If the swelling doesn't go down, we'll have the vet come out and take a look."

The trailer was big enough that Jane could go inside with Starlight, so she took the reins and led the horse into the trailer. Once the horse was secured inside, Jane got out and helped George put away the ramp and lock the doors. They turned to Carol, and both thanked her again for her help. She waved it off.

"Think nothing of it. I'll look forward to seeing you again soon," she said to Jane. "Drive safely."

George and Jane got into the jeep and headed home.

"Carol and her husband just moved to town a week ago, so they don't know anyone. She said that I'm the first person that she's really had a chance to talk with. I'm sorry that Starlight got hurt, but I'm glad that I was able to met Carol," said Jane.

"She seems really nice. Did you meet her husband?"

"No, he's not here yet. He has to finish up his notice in Texas before he can come. That's part of the reason she was happy I came by."

They discussed the possibility that Starlight might have sprained her ankle but dismissed it as unlikely.

When they got home, they unloaded Starlight and put her in her stall. Then they unhitched the trailer from the jeep and put the jeep back inside the garage.

"I'm sorry you had to come get me," Jane said.

"That's okay. You called at a good time." He put his arm around her shoulders and gave her a side hug.

All the lights in the house were off except in the family room. While Jane went to bed, George went to see if his parents were in the room. Sitting on the couch with her back to him, her knees propping up a Bible, was Alex. She was so engrossed in what she was reading that she didn't realize George was there until he came into her line of sight.

"George!" she said, quickly closing the book and standing up. "You're back already?"

"So it seems. What are you reading?"

"Oh, I hope you don't mind. I found your Bible and thought I'd take a look." She shifted nervously from one foot to the other.

"I don't mind at all. What I meant was what part are you reading?"

"Oh. The part where the woman washes Jesus' feet."

"Good part. I think my favorite New Testament story is the one where Christ, then Peter, walks on the water. I think it shows that even the most impossible things can become possible, with enough faith. Faith in yourself, and in Heavenly Father."

"I haven't read the Bible or been to church since high school. I did it then because it was expected. It didn't matter what church, but I had to go every week."

"If you'd like, I'll read a bit with you," George offered.

"No, I think I'll just go to bed. I'm really tired."

63

"Sure, no problem. I need to do the same. I'll walk you to your room."

At her door Alex turned to him. "Thanks for today. I had a lot of fun."

"I'm glad. I like to see you laugh. Your eyes sparkle and you look like… Well, I haven't quite figured out what you make me think of, but I like it," he said, smiling slightly.

Alex blushed but smiled before opening the door and stepping inside.

George went to bed happy at the progress he saw Alex making.

The next morning George beat Alex to breakfast. Cherish had started breakfast but had stepped away. George picked up the glass of juice that was waiting for him and took a couple of sips. For not getting much sleep, he felt energized, alive in a way that he hadn't been since his mission for the church when he was nineteen.

Still in his nightclothes, he decided that he would cook breakfast for Alex. He got out a couple of eggs and some bacon and mushrooms. He started the bacon and mushrooms cooking while he beat the eggs. He flipped the bacon over and added the eggs. He spread some refried beans and cheese on a tortilla and put it in the microwave. While the tortilla was heating, he folded the omelet in half. Once the tortilla was ready, he added some ranch dressing and guacamole, then placed the omelet on top of everything. He folded the tortilla and set it on a plate. He found another bottle of cherries, opened it, and poured half the cherries into a bowl, which he set next to the plate with the burrito. He squeezed more oranges and added a glass of juice to the rest of the food on the table. After making his own breakfast burrito and pouring the rest of the cherries for himself, George went to Alex's room and knocked softly on the door.

"Coming," she croaked.

When she opened the door, George almost swallowed his tongue. She was beautiful during the day, but having just gotten out of bed, she looked like a little lost girl. The only thing missing was a teddy bear or blankey. Her hair was mussed and her eyes were full of sleep, and she was wearing a knee-length nightgown with a sleeping Mickey Mouse on it. Around Mickey were the words, 'Do not disturb, sweet dreams in progress'. Somehow, despite the fact that the kiddy nightgown made her look like a little girl, she was absolutely, jaw-droppingly gorgeous.

Once he remembered how to breathe again, he said, "I made breakfast for you. It's ready."

"Just give me a minute," she said, rubbing her eyes, then yawning.

George's feet felt like they were going to grow roots, and he had to force himself to move away.

"I'll see you in the kitchen in a bit, then," he said, forcing himself to not turn around and go back to her.

In the kitchen, he quickly blessed his food and then gulped down his juice. He sat there, stunned by how much he had wanted to take Alex in his arms and never let her go. Between the little girl look of her in her nightclothes and the woman he knew her to be, it was getting harder and harder to not hold her to him forever.

Alex came in a few minutes later, her hair smoothed down, wearing a soft, light blue robe and fluffy pink bunny slippers. George eyed the slippers, and quirked an eyebrow.

"What? They keep my feet warm and they're cute. Closest thing to a pet I have right now, and I don't have to clean up after them," Alex said nonchalantly.

"Nothing. Just not the sort of slippers I'd have thought you'd wear, that's all. Although, maybe I shouldn't be so surprised considering what you wear to bed," he said, smiling.

Ignoring his comment about her sleepwear, she asked, "Do you have any coffee? I stayed up late reading."

"Sorry. We don't drink coffee. I squeezed you some o.j. though."

"That's okay. I've been trying to cut back. Coffee has a tendency to make me hyper, and I've decided that hyper's not the best thing in the world first thing in the morning."

Alex sat down and bowed her head. George watched in fascination at her progress. She had been with them for less than three full days and she'd gone from apparently not having much to do with religion in several years, to reading the scriptures and blessing her food. It was really amazing how things worked out, if you let them.

After she blessed her food, Alex drank half her juice in one go. Then she took a big bite of her breakfast burrito. After swallowing, she finished off her juice.

"George, this is wonderful. Did your mom teach you how to make this?"

"No. Well, she showed me the basics of the burrito, but I added my own twist with the guacamole and the ranch. I'm glad you like it."

"Like it? I love it. You'll have to show me how to make it. Knowing how to make two breakfasts will definitely help me to start eating better."

"Not a problem, I'd love to show you."

They ate heartily in silence, both of them enjoying the good food and one another's company. They were just about to leave the kitchen when Cherish came in and picked up the phone, a concerned look on her face.

"What's wrong?" George asked.

"It's Starlight's leg. Jane came in from feeding the horses and asked me to take a look at it. I'd better give the vet a call and have her come take a look since it's still swollen from last night," she said as she punched in the numbers for the vet.

George and Alex stood there listening as Cherish made the phone call.

"She said she'll be here as soon as she can, probably in about half an hour," Cherish said after she hung up the phone.

"Did Vici say there was anything we should do in the meantime?" George asked.

"Just make sure Starlight isn't putting any weight on the leg."

George and Alex quickly went to throw on some clothes, then hurried to the barn to wait for the vet. Jane was in the stall petting the horse's head, trying to keep her calm.

They had only been waiting a few minutes before a serious-looking woman only a few years older than George came into the barn. She wore a plaid shirt, well-worn blue jeans, and cowboy boots. Her long brown hair was French-braided and hung down her back. The woman walked straight to them, carrying an old-fashioned doctor's bag in one hand. She went into the stall without a word to anyone, and set her bag down by the door. She knelt next

66

to Starlight and felt down the horse's left back leg, testing the foot's range of motion.

"I doubt that anything's broken, but I do think she's got a bad sprain." Looking at Jane she asked, "You were riding her?"

"Yes, last night."

"In the future, don't ride after dark, especially in the snow."

Looking at her feet Jane mumbled, "Yes, ma'am."

Vici kept looking at Jane until Jane finally looked up. Jane looked into Vici's eyes for a moment and then repeated what she had said more firmly. Satisfied with Jane's response, Vici stood up, and dusted off her hands.

Pulling a bottle of pills from her bag, she said, "I'll give her some bute to help with the inflammation and pain. If she doesn't start showing improvement in the next three days, give me a call. That's all I can do for now. Jane, you need to make sure she takes it easy. Absolutely no riding until her leg's better.

"Cherish, I'll send you a bill. Hope you folks have a good day. I'll see you later."

Alex stood there slightly stunned while everyone else went about their various activities. George gave the injured horse a couple of handfuls of oats, while Jane crooned to her. Cherish gave all three horses a lump of sugar from a plastic container she pulled off a shelf.

"Who was that whirlwind?" Alex asked, recovering from the abruptness of the visit.

"Oh, that was Vici. She's always like that," said Cherish. "She does seem to blow in and out, doesn't she?"

"Remind me to never be in her way when she's doing that," said Alex.

The others laughed. George had known Vici since they were kids. Vici was a few years older than he was, and at one time she had babysat for his parents on the few occasions when they had gone into town for a meeting or something and didn't want to take the kids with them. She'd been abrupt then, too, almost militaristic in her mannerisms.

"You spend enough time around her and you get used to it," he said.

After petting Charlie and Cinder for a few minutes, everyone but Jane left the barn and walked back to the house.

Cherish said she was going to go visit some of the women from church.

Once in the house George said, "I'm going to work in the darkroom for a while, Alex. I hope you don't mind if I leave you to your own devices."

"No, that's fine. I'll find something to do."

George went to the darkroom and developing the second roll of film. Once the film was to a safe point in the processing, he started to examine the pictures from the first roll. He found the ones he thought they could use, and began enlarging them. He had just hung up the last one when there was a knock on the outer door.

"Come in," he called.

He heard the door open and close before Alex opened the second door.

"Hey, you have to come see these," he said excitedly.

Alex walked the few steps to where George stood and looked at the prints that were hung up to dry. Then she started to laugh. George had captured the moment when one of Nancy's snowballs had caught Jane on the side of her face, and the look of cold shock on Jane's face was priceless.

"That was a good one," Alex said, laughing. "Jane had just stood up from getting new snow and didn't see it coming. How much longer is it going to take you to finish up here?"

"A few hours still. Should have them all ready tonight. Did you just come to check on my progress?"

"No, I came to tell you that lunch is ready. Can you leave, or should we save some for you?"

"I can come now. Let me wash up first and I'll be there in about five minutes."

Alex left and George put a few things away before going to wash his hands.

Over lunch, George asked Alex what she had done to keep occupied while he had been in the darkroom.

"I tinkered around on the piano a bit and then Jane and I played a game of Sorry!."

Jane, sitting at the table as well, piped up. "Yup, we played Sorry!, but I don't think I've come across anyone who's less sorry. Not even you have her beat for competitiveness. Remind me never to play a game with just the two of us again!"

They all laughed, and George said, "Thanks for the head's up. Now I have an idea of what I'd be up against."

They laughed and joked about the day while they ate. Once they had finished lunch, George and Jane taught Alex a card game, which they played until George announced that he needed to get back to the darkroom and finish the pictures. He emerged shortly before dinner, and he and Alex went into his dad's office to look at the prints.

They sat next to each other on the loveseat and looked over the two dozen or so pictures that George thought might work.

"I really like these," she said, indicating a couple of pictures. "I think there are some really good ones here."

"Thank you," he said.

They settled on three that they wanted to try in the layout. While they scanned in the photos, George asked more about her time with Mrs. Hagerman.

"You've been with Mrs. H for six months, right?" he asked.

"Yes, about that."

"What did you do before she hired you?"

"I mentioned being in Houston and Vegas. I found a job in Vegas that was kind of like what I've been doing for Mrs. Hagerman, but for less pay and less time for myself. I heard through the grapevine that Mrs. Hagerman was looking for someone with experience, someone who, once they were told what to do, would just do it, and solve any problems that came up along the way. I hadn't had the kind of experience I thought I should have had to be hired, but Mrs. Hagerman must have thought I had potential. After only one interview, she said she wanted me."

"I know how she can be about running her place. Was it hard for you to figure out how you needed to do things?"

"You bet it was hard. My predecessor had left things in a mess. She'd eloped with Mrs. Hagerman's chauffeur and decided to not come back. Anyway, Mrs. Hagerman did take some pity on me, because she had one of the secretaries help me until I straightened things out. After that, I just had to try and think like she did, and ask for help from those who'd been around a while. I think I'm finally getting the hang of working for her, though, or I don't think she would have sent me to help you with this layout."

"Does she ever make you feel like a child who's just been caught raiding the cookie jar?"

"Only when something happens that shouldn't have and I was involved. Just after I got there, she asked me to order new stationery. Somehow the order got mixed up, and we were sent stationery that had flowers all over it. I was with her when she opened it. She gave me one look, and I felt like I had when my mom discovered that I'd popped the tops off her tulips before they'd bloomed. Before she had a chance to say anything, I told her that I would have the correct order shipped the next day. She nodded once and left the room. I tell you, I don't think I've ever dialed a phone number as fast as I did that day."

The pictures finished scanning, so they turned their attention to the computer. They looked at all the pictures from the ski slope and decided on two that they might be able to use.

While they were finalizing their choices, the bell rang for dinner. Dinner was once again a pleasant time and George was happy to see that Alex looked totally relaxed and comfortable with his family. After dinner, Jane announced that she needed to get ready for a date, and she didn't know when she'd be back. George and Alex returned to the office and continued to work on the layout. But George got distracted when Alex asked him when he got started on photography.

"I started taking pictures when I was about six or seven. My mom had just gotten a new camera, so she gave me her old one. I'd go around the house and catch everyone doing whatever. After getting a picture of my dad in the bathroom, I wasn't allowed to take pictures for a month. I was always careful after that that my 'subjects' weren't doing something that they wouldn't want to see later. Well, most of the time I was careful," he said, smiling.

"Did you do anything with photography in high school?"

"I was on the yearbook committee, all four years. I also was hired every once in a while to take pictures for my friends' siblings' birthday parties and such. In college I took a couple of photography classes, including one on photojournalism, and I really thought I'd found what I wanted to do. I was going to be the one taking pictures of places and things that people either hadn't seen before or that I thought they should see. After my mission for our church, I was finishing up my degree and met Pat. He thought that with his business degree and my artistic sense, we should open up our own advertising business. I prayed about it for quite a while before feeling I felt like that was the right thing to do. So we got our degrees, and after a couple of hard years, things started falling into place."

"You said that you prayed to find out if the ad agency was the right thing for you. How did you know that was the right thing to do?"

"Well, two things happened. The first was that I was able to talk with a guy who'd done photojournalism for over twenty years. He helped me realize that even though I might be bringing a bit of the world to people, I would have to travel more than I might really want to, and in the end, that I'd probably miss out on things that would be more important. Also, I might have to do things that were very unpleasant, maybe even against my religion, in order to get close to people--like smoking a peace pipe.

"The second thing that happened was that I was able to intern for a successful ad agency. I was able to use my creativity and camera skills to help companies strike the right chord with the public. It gave me a thrill to come up with just the right slogan, or jingle, or whatever, that I decided that, although I'd still like to travel some day, that day wasn't there yet."

"Do you often pray about what you're going to do?"

"Whenever I feel I need the extra help. I can't see the big picture, but Heavenly Father can. I know that he helps guide me, even in small things, if I ask. There's a quote I found somewhere that I really like: 'The time may be delayed, the manner may be unexpected, but the answer is sure to come. Not a tear of sacred sorrow, not a breath of holy desire poured out to God will ever be lost, but in God's own time and way will be wafted back again in clouds of mercy, and fall in showers of blessing on you and on those for whom you pray.'

"He will answer our prayers, but like the quote says, it's not always how or when we want it. It's up to us to be listening for it and to accept it when it comes."

"You've really given me things to think about. I'm glad that I've had a chance to get to know you like this. I wonder if we'd met at the office how things would have turned out between us?" she said thoughtfully. "Oh, well. It didn't, and we have pictures to work on. We'd better get going. I'd like to be able to call Mrs. Hagerman tomorrow and see what she thinks."

They worked a bit longer until the bell for scriptures rang. Alex joined them, but decided to just listen. Once scriptures were done, they went back to the office and printed a test copy of the brochure.

Alex said, "You know, Mrs. Hagerman was right to insist that you do this. These pictures are really amazing. You've managed to capture the energy and enjoyment of the skiers. And Jane took some pretty good pictures, too. I know Mrs. Hagerman will be happy with these, I'd stake my next raise on it. Now let me email her the file and I'll give her a call in the morning."

The next morning when George walked into the kitchen, he asked Alex if she had called Mrs. H. yet. Alex said she had wanted to wait until he was up. They went into the office and she made the call. Alex asked if Mrs. Hagerman wanted anything tweaked. Five minutes later Alex and George were congratulating each other on a job well done.

"Mrs. Hagerman said she liked it so well and that I've worked so hard these last few months, that she wants me to take the next week off, till just after Christmas!" Alex said, jumping up and down like a child.

"That's great, Alex. I'm happy that you get to take some time off. What are you going to do?" George asked, his heart in his throat.

"I'm not sure. Maybe I should visit my family. I haven't really kept in touch with them, and maybe I should make more of an effort."

"I'm sure they would like that. But if you decide that you'd rather, I'm sure you can stay here a bit longer. After all, we're just getting to know you, and my parents would love to have someone else here for Christmas," he said as calmly as he could.

For some reason, he felt that if she left now, the progress she had made would not continue. And as much as he wanted her to spend time with her family, he wanted her to stay with them, if only for a little bit longer.

"Actually, I would like to stay, if for no other reason than to be around a real family again."

"Then it's settled. You'll stay here until you have to go back. I'll see if I can talk Mrs. H. into letting you go visit your family sometime in the spring," he said quickly.

"I really appreciate the gesture, but I don't know how I feel about your doing that. Not right now, anyway."

"I'll go with whatever you decide," he assured her. "How about celebrating?"

"With what?"

"I'll make a batch of German apple cider."

"What makes that any different from normal cider?"

"Ah! Now that's a secret, at least for now. Let go to the kitchen and make sure Mom has everything we'll need."

They went to the kitchen, and without giving anything away, he checked to see if they had what they would need. George poked around and found that they did have everything. He pulled out a five-quart crock-pot and poured most of a gallon of apple juice into it.

"Okay, we need ten sticks of cinnamon, allspice, and whole cloves," he told her.

After putting the spices in a cheesecloth pouch, George told Alex that she had to leave while he put the 'secret' ingredients in. Alex went along with little game and went to play the piano. While she was gone, George got out the rest of the ingredients and put them in the crock-pot. He then filled the crock-pot to the top with more apple juice, turned the crock-pot to high, and went to join Alex.

In the front room, Alex was trying to play a song. From her posture and manner, George could tell that it was one she was unfamiliar with.

"Would you like me to play it for you?" he asked.

"Sure. Are there any lyrics with it?"

"Yes. Want me to sing it, too?"

"That would be great. It looks like a really neat song."

George took Alex's place at piano and started playing the intro with a flourish. Then he settled down to play the song. As he started to sing, the music and words spoke of Christ and his mission. It spoke of a man watching Christ as he preformed miracles, healing the sick, helping the lame to walk. It spoke of Gethsemane, of his being scourged, and finally, nailed to the cross.

Although the song sounded like it was going to end there, it continued on to Christ's resurrection and the hope for repentance and eternal life that is given to all who believe on His name. George sang the last refrain with such force, such knowledge that what he was singing was true, that he almost choked on the words as the Spirit witnessed in his heart that what he was singing was, indeed, true.

When he finished, he turned to Alex and could tell by the look in her eyes that she had felt the Spirit, too.

"We haven't really talked about this before, but do you know what that is that you feel, in your heart?"

"How do you know that I feel something?" she asked, somewhat astonished.

"Because I feel it, too, and I can see it in your face. Anytime I hear or read something that is spiritually true, I feel like this--sometimes more strongly than at other times, but I always feel like my heart is being warmed by the Spirit."

"Is that the Holy Spirit, then? I've heard people say they've felt the Spirit, but they were never able to tell me how they felt it."

"Yes, that's the Holy Ghost. Not everyone feels it in the same way, and sometimes the same person will feel it differently in different situations. It's also called 'the still small voice' because of the quiet way it can put thoughts into our mind and heart."

As she didn't seem to have anything more to say just then, he let the topic go.

"Do you want to do something else while the cider is heating up?" he asked.

"Sure. What do you have in mind?"

"We could play a game. My parents have a huge game closet."

They went to the closet and Alex gasped when she saw how full it was.

"It looks like you could open your own game store! I don't think I've ever known anyone with this many games."

George laughed. "Yes, they do have quite a few. We had so many friends over when we were growing up, that my parents thought it would be a good idea to have enough to do to keep us out of trouble. It became a joke that if any of our friends were bored, they'd come over here to find a game to play."

After a few minutes they decided on Monopoly and went into the kitchen to set it up.

"What do you want to be?" he asked her.

"I like being the car. It's the fastest piece so it zooms past the competition. What about you?" she asked as she took the game piece.

"I like the iron. You may try to zoom past everyone, but I flatten them."

Once they had the money counted out and were ready to start, they rolled to see who would go first. George rolled first.

"Snake eyes. Dang. I should get to try again. There's nothing that's worse. I should have a fair shake," he wheedled.

"Nope. One roll and one roll only," she said as she picked up the dice. "Double sixes! See, you wouldn't have beaten that if you had re-rolled."

As they played, they each picked up property and razzed one another about not doing better. As they neared 'Go' a few rounds later, Alex managed to land on both Park Place and Boardwalk.

George started to complain that Alex had cheated, grinning to let her know he wasn't serious.

"You call me a cheat when I know that you're the one who sneaks looks at his sister's tiles in Scrabble?"

George had the grace to look ashamed and didn't try to deny it.

They played a few more rounds when they heard a car pull into the garage.

"Mom must be home," George said as he paid Alex for landing on one of her railroads.

Cherish came in a few minutes later carrying a couple grocery bags. George quickly got up to help her.

"Thanks, sweetheart," she said, and then sniffed. "You're making cider, aren't you? That's perfect, then. I was going to make it up before I left, but I forgot. Have you had any yet?"

"No. We got caught up in the game and haven't even checked it," Alex told her. "Besides, your son doesn't seem to think I should know what the 'secret' ingredients are."

"I'm sure it'll be worth the wait. I'll check it and let you know if it's ready," Cherish offered.

She got out a ladle and a mug. After pouring herself some of the drink, she took a sip.

"Mmm. This is perfect," she said, taking out the cheesecloth pouch that held the spices. "Here, Alex, I'll pour you some. See if you can tell what we put in it that makes it so good."

Alex took a cautious sip, then another, then drank half the glass.

"Wow, this is wonderful. I taste orange, a little lemon, and…" She took another sip and frowned. "I'm not quite sure what the other flavor is."

"It's lime," George said.

"That is so cool. I would never have thought to put citrus fruits in cider. How did you come up with that?"

"We had some really good friends who'd lived in Germany for a while. When they came back, they shared some of the culture and food with us. This is one of the things they showed us," Cherish told her.

"I did tell you that it was 'German' apple cider," he said, smiling.

George went over to the cupboards, pulled out a glass, and poured some cider for each of them.

After handing Cherish and Alex their mugs he said, "I propose a toast. To new friends, and getting the layout done."

Alex and Cherish repeated the toast and they all clinked their mugs together.

When they had drained their glasses, and George refilled them before he and Alex sat down to finish the game.

Half an hour later they gave up all pretenses of trying to win the game, and started goofing off. George flattened the board with his iron, and Alex zoomed around it with her car.

Laughing, Alex said, "I don't know the last time I've had as much fun as I've had since coming here. I don't know if I've ever laughed this much at all."

As they put the game away George said, "Growing up, it was like this a lot. Even though Mom is pretty strict most of the time and doesn't let things slide, she always had time to joke around with us. And Dad was always kidding with us, trying to get our goat. Fortunately, he's mellowed some. I'm really glad they taught us that a sense of humor was very important. Mom says that's part of her secret for looking ten years younger than she is."

"I wondered about that," said Alex. "I know that as you get older, age gaps don't seem to matter as much, but she does look quite a bit younger than your dad does."

"And the funny thing about that is that she's two years older than he is."

They continued to chat as they put the game back in the closet. After closing the door, they looked at each other for a moment. George looked at her questioningly, and Alex looked back with uncertainty in her eyes. Neither could put the question or answer into words at the moment, but each understood the other. Then George smiled and the moment was lost. But he felt he had at least part of the answer he had been looking for.

"What would you like to do now?" he asked.

"I don't know. Why don't we see if Nancy wants to do something?"

George called up Nancy. She said she would love to get together as she was going a little stir crazy at the moment. They decided to meet at Nancy's house a half hour later.

Alex picked out tunes on the piano while George called Pat from the office extension. Pat picked up on the third ring.

"Pat Michael speaking."

"Hey, Pat. It's George. How's it going in sunny So. Cal?"

"It's fine. We just finished up the Collins account and are about ready to submit our proposal for the Smyth account. How about you? How are you and Alex hitting it off? Any sparks yet?"

"You are one sneaky... I don't know what, but you're sneaky. Is there some reason you didn't correct my assumption that Alex was a guy?"

"Of course there is. I wanted her to catch you off-guard," Pat said, chuckling. "You always seem to have the upper hand, and I thought it was time someone else did, if only for a few seconds. So, how do you like her?"

"She's nice enough," George said, downplaying his feelings. He wasn't about to give Pat a chance to gloat until he had to. "Mom invited her to stay with us. Mrs. H. was so pleased with what we sent her, and with Alex's own hard work, that she has given Alex till just after Christmas off."

"Methinks there's more going on than you're letting on, but I'll let it pass. Too hard to get it out of you over the phone," said Pat.

"You wouldn't be able to get anything else out of me if you were here, anyway. Hey, I have to go. We're going over to Nancy's house to bum around."

After they said their good-byes, George hung up the phone, a thoughtful expression on his face. He left to get Alex.

Chapter 6

At Nancy's house they parked the car in the driveway. After a perfunctory knock, George opened the door and announced their arrival.

"Come on in. I'll be down in a minute," Nancy called from upstairs.

When Nancy came downstairs, George and Alex both looked at her with concern.

"Nan, you look pale. Are you sure you're up for company?" George asked, going over to take her arm and help her sit down on the sofa.

Nancy put one hand to her forehead and the other to her stomach.

"I don't know. Just a few minutes ago I started to feel dizzy and sick to my stomach. I was trying to rest till you got here, but I don't think that's helped."

"When was the last time you ate," Alex asked, sitting down on the other side of Nancy.

"I think I had some juice this morning. I was about to start breakfast when I had a phone call from one of the ladies at church.

She just had a c-section and her six-year-old twin boys had decided that jumping out of a tree was a good idea. One of them broke his arm and she needed me to take him to the hospital. After I brought him home, she asked me to stay with her for a bit to talk. I'd just gotten home when you called."

Looking at his watch, George was surprised to find that it was almost dinnertime.

"Nancy, we're going to get you some food. You just lie down and rest," he said. "Alex, will you get her an ice pack out of the freezer? I'll show you where the tea towels are."

Once Nancy was lying down with an ice pack on her forehead, Alex went into the kitchen to see what there was to cook. Alex found George at the stove, opening a quart jar of homemade chicken soup. While he poured the contents of the jar into a pot, she got out the makings for ham sandwiches. They worked in harmony preparing a light dinner for Nancy. Once it was done, they loaded it onto a tray and took it out to her. Alex helped Nancy sit up, then George placed the tray on her lap.

"Thank you, guys. This looks so good. I'm sorry I'm being such a poor hostess. Here you are, cooking the food for me," she said weakly as she picked up the glass of water on the tray.

"Nonsense," Alex told her. "We're only too happy to help. I know what it's like being sick and not having anyone around to help. It's no fun having to cook your own food when you'd rather be lying down. You just eat up. We'll stick around until your husband comes home."

"Yes, how would Doug feel if we just left you alone? He might come over and beat me up, or something. Wouldn't want to go around with a broken nose for not helping you," he said, trying to lighten her mood.

After taking a sip of water, Nancy looked at them.

"Thank you, anyway. I'll eat this then go upstairs. Feel free to watch a movie or something. And eat, yourselves. Wouldn't want you getting faint because you helped me," she said with a weak smile.

George and Alex went into the kitchen to help themselves to the rest of the food they had prepared. They sat down at the table, George blessing the food, then they started to eat.

After eating for a bit, Alex commented, "This is the best chicken soup I've ever had. Your mom made it, right?"

Chucking, he said, "You guessed it. Mom had invited them over for dinner a while ago, but they couldn't make it, so she canned some for them. She figures that you never know when you'll get sick or need a quick meal. As usual, she's right."

As they continued to eat in silence, George marveled at how comfortable he was with Alex. He didn't feel the need to fill the void, as he did with some women, and Alex didn't seem too either. Whether they were laughing, riding, playing games, playing the piano, or whatever, he never felt anything but happy to be with Alex. And watching her help take care of Nancy made him think of what it would be like to have her help take care of their own children. He liked the feeling this thought brought. As he looked at her, he realized that he loved her. He didn't just want her taking care of their children, he wanted to take care of her. Help her to laugh and have fun, help her to overcome the sorrows in life. He wanted to show her forever, not for just a few weeks, what a loving family was. His heart felt so full of love for her he thought it was going to choke him. Tears came to his eyes. He blinked the tears away, took a deep breath, then released it.

At his sigh, Alex looked up, a questioning look in her eyes. George just shook his head, a big smile on his face, and she went back to her dinner, taking the last bite of her sandwich. George finished his own in two bites and stood up to clear away the dishes. While he was doing that, Alex left the room, and George could hear her talking with Nancy. She brought in Nancy's tray, frowning at how little had been eaten.

"I wonder if Nancy is sicker than we thought?" Alex said.

"I'm sure she'll be fine. We'll let Doug know when he gets home and he can keep an eye on her."

"I'm going to help her upstairs. Do you want to start a movie?"

"Sure. I'll see you in the living room in a minute."

In the living room he looked at the movies. He pulled out one of his favorite love stories. It wasn't something he'd tell his pals, but he liked a good romance once in a while.

The movie was just starting when Alex came down. She sat down a little ways from George, took off her shoes, and tucked her feet up next to her. When she realized what the movie was, she raised an eyebrow at him, but George only shrugged.

By the end of the movie, the room was dark except for the TV. Alex and George were cuddled next to each other, Alex all but asleep, George trying to smooth her curls. Her hair was as soft as he had thought it would be, and the curls seemed to want to twine around his fingers. They heard the door open, and George hugged Alex quickly before stretching. Alex followed his example, yawning widely at the end of her stretch.

"Nancy, I'm home," Doug called out, just like in the TV shows from the '50s. He flipped on the light in the hall.

"We're in here," George called out, walking over to the doorway. "Nancy's upstairs; she wasn't feeling well."

Walking into the living room Doug said, "George! I thought that was your jeep in the drive. She's okay, isn't she?"

"Yes, she's fine. She hadn't eaten much since this morning, so we got her some food and put her to bed," Alex said.

Going over to Alex, Doug held out his hand. "You must be Alex. I've heard quite a bit about you from Nancy. I'm glad you were here to help."

Alex took his hand and shook it. "It was my pleasure. I'm glad I was here when she needed someone."

"We wanted to make sure you knew that even though Nancy hadn't eaten much today, she didn't eat much dinner, either. It could be the flu or a stomach bug. Let us know how she is tomorrow," George said, as he turned off the TV and headed for the front door. Doug followed them to the door.

"I will. And thanks for staying with her. I'll talk with you tomorrow."

George and Alex left the house and got in the jeep. As they drove back to the Hart house, George wanted to shout for joy. He loved Alex and he knew that he had to tell her, but for the moment, he was content to hug his secret to himself. He knew that when he told her, he wanted it to be special, but comfortable. As they chatted about the movie they had watched, he started planning how and when he would propose.

Back at the house Jane and Cherish were in the kitchen getting some plates of cookies together.

"Do you want to come with us?" Jane asked Alex. "We're planning on doing knock-n-runs to seven or eight houses."

"I've never heard of that before. What do you do?" Alex asked.

"You go up to a house, set the plate on the doorstep, ring the bell or knock, then run like the dickens so that when they open the door, they don't know who was there," George told her. "It's a lot of fun, if tiring. We like to go to families from church that have a lot of kids, or who are older and by themselves. The kids love to try and figure out who was there, the older folks like to know that someone remembers them."

"I'm not sure if I'm up to doing it myself, but I'll go for the fun of watching you guys run," Alex said, smiling.

"Okay, then. Alex and George, if you'll help us wrap these plates up, we'll be on our way in a few minutes," said Cherish.

"What about Dad?" George asked, as he tucked plastic wrap around a paper plate.

"He had a meeting he had to go to and said for us to not wait for him," his mother replied.

After all the plates were assembled, Cherish drove them to the various houses. She would park the car either down the street or around the corner while George and Jane took turns leaving plates of cookies on the doorsteps. At one house, George had to dive into the bushes to avoid being spotted when the door opened sooner than he expected. The shouts of joy from the child who had answered the door were all the reward he needed to make up for the scratches he received.

At the last house, George turned to Alex and said, "Okay, this one's yours. You've spent the last half hour laughing at us for almost getting caught and coming back out of breath. I think turnabout is fair play."

As he leaned over and opened her door for her, Alex protested, but George could tell that it was only for form's sake. She got out and took the last plate from Jane. After being told which house to go to, Alex shut the car door and started down the street.

George, Jane, and Cherish all watched as Alex sneaked up to the house, being careful to stay out of any direct light. She set the plate down as carefully as she could, stood up, and was about to ring the bell when the door suddenly opened. An old grizzled man of about eighty stood there, frowning at her. George could see in the set of Alex's shoulders her indecision as to whether to run or admit she'd been caught leaving cookies. Good manners must have won out, because she picked up the plate and handed it to the man. George could see the smile that split his face as he realized her purpose in being there. He talked to her for a few seconds, before gesturing for her to go inside. Her shoulders relaxed and she shook her head, pointing back to the car. The old man laughed, then motioned to those in the car for them to join Alex and him.

Cherish laughed, breaking the silence that had fallen as they watched to see what would happen. She unbuckled and got out of the car. Jane and George followed her example. When they got close to the house, the old man called out to them in a voice that sounded much younger than he looked.

"So you're the rapscallions that made this purdy young thing come over here. I'd whup ya for it, but she made me promise not to," he said, the twinkle in his eyes shining even in the dim light. "Since I caught her out, I think it only fair that y'all come in and set a spell."

"Brother Carmichael, we'd love to come in," Cherish accepted. "And George is the rapscallion, so whatever punishment you have for him, it's probably fitting."

Brother Carmichael stood to the side as they entered the front room. The house was well kept, if in need of new carpet and wallpaper, not having been replaced since the late '70s. George knew from experience that it was the efforts of Sister Carmichael that kept the place so tidy. Brother Carmichael said that if it weren't for her, the place would look like a bachelor pad. And even though they had had the opportunity to have new carpet and wallpaper installed, Sister Carmichael wouldn't have the house any other way. She stated that until the floor underneath could be seen, the carpet would stay, and that the wallpaper would last a long time yet if taken care of.

Brother Carmichael led them to a worn lime green sofa and asked them to sit. He then went to find Sister Carmichael. When they came back, they both were carrying trays, one with the cookies, divided up onto smaller plates, and the other with glasses of milk. They set the trays down on a coffee table that looked even older than the carpet and sofa, and then sat down on a matching loveseat.

"Please, have some cookies and milk," Sister Carmichael said, her voice as sweet and youthful as a young bride's.

Dutifully obeying, they each took a plate and glass, even Cherish.

"It was so nice of you to think of us this year," Sister Carmichael told Cherish. "But our health isn't as good as we'd like it, and, as much as we would like to eat these cookies, they wouldn't agree with us. So we'll enjoy watching you enjoy them, if you don't mind."

"Not at all, Sister Carmichael. It was silly of me not to check first and find out what you would prefer to have."

"What we'd prefer is the company that you've brought with the cookies," Brother Carmichael said, taking his wife's hand.

As the four of them ate cookies and drank milk, Brother and Sister Carmichael chatted with them. They wanted to know about Alex, how long she was to be in town, how long George had known her, and if they were dating.

At the last question, Alex and George looked at one another, Alex looking away first. George again cursed his tendency to blush easily.

"I'm not sure if we are dating, but I know I'd like to," he said, and was rewarded when he saw Alex blush lightly, too.

Alex, meanwhile, made a point of brushing all the crumbs in her lap back onto her plate before setting it as gently as she could on the coffee table. She then finished off her milk and put the glass down as well.

The others took this in with much interest, but politely refrained from commenting on the exchange.

When Jane finished her snack, set her dishes on one of the trays, and then gathered up the rest of the dishes. As she stood up, tray in hand, Sister Carmichael stood up, too.

"Oh, dear, don't do that. I'll take care of the dishes. You sit down and rest. Knowing you, you've done a few knock-n-runs tonight."

"No, Sister Carmichael, I'll take care of them, at least as far as taking them to the kitchen. I know you've worked hard all your life, so you just sit back down and let someone else to a bit of the work for a change," she said politely, but firmly.

Sister Carmichael sank back down and then said, "You are a dear, and a credit to your mother. Have it your way. Go ahead and just set them next to the sink."

After a few more minutes, Cherish said they had to go. At the front door they each in turn gave Sister Carmichael a hug and shook Brother Carmichael's hand.

"You feel free to come back any time, Miss," Brother Carmichael told Alex.

"Yes, dear, we'd like to see you again, if you don't mind. You can bring George or Jane with you, if you'd like. Our children are too far away to visit often, and they all have large families. It's hard on us to have young children running around when they do come, so it'd be nice to have some young people in the house that we don't have to watch out for."

"I'd like that," she said, smiling.

Back in the car they all laughed about what had happened. George was glad that Alex had enjoyed her visit with the Carmichaels and hoped she would visit them again. They enjoyed having visitors, but rarely had any other than a few people from church.

When they got home, they went into the kitchen and found Kurt enjoying a mug of cider. Everyone agreed that having cider would be a great way to end the evening, so they warmed some up before going to read scriptures. This time Alex even took a turn at reading. The look of contentment on her face made George glad that he was able to help her overcome some of her demons, and he looked forward to slaying a few more. As they knelt for the prayer, Alex hesitantly asked if she could be allowed to offer the prayer. George knew his parents well enough to know that although they didn't show it outwardly, they were somewhat surprised by the request. Kurt nodded his head before readying himself for the prayer.

Alex's prayer showed her growing understanding of Heavenly Father's love for her and her growing love for those that knelt with her. She expressed her gratitude for the time she was being able to spend with them and all that they were helping her to learn. She asked that their friendships would continue past the holidays, and that they would all have a good night's rest. As they stood up, Kurt thanked Alex for giving such a heartfelt prayer.

"Thank you for letting me say it," Alex said. "I haven't said a prayer out loud since I left home. I felt that it was time that I did it again. I didn't realize how much I missed it. Besides, I really wanted you all to know how much your compassion and understanding has meant to me."

Cherish went over to Alex and gave her a hug. As she did so, the tears that had been in Alex's voice gave way. The two women stood there for a minute, Cherish giving Alex the love of a mother to a child that's just come home from a long time away, Alex crying slightly for the love of a family after so many years without one. When Alex finally pulled away, she laughed shakily as she wiped the tears from her face.

"I don't quite know why I'm being so silly. I haven't cried in too long to be doing it now."

"Sometimes it's because it's been so long, that we cry," Cherish wisely told Alex, patting her on the cheek.

"Well, I need to get to bed," Kurt said, stretching. "I've got a busy day tomorrow. Are you coming, dearheart?"

"I'll be there in a minute," Cherish said. The special smile on her face let everyone know that she still loved her husband very much.

"Jane, will you sit on the porch with me?" Alex asked.

"Sure. I'll grab a blanket and meet you out there."

George just stood there as the rest of his family left the room. The love he had started to feel for Alex grew as he went over what had just happened. He felt even more certain than he had at Doug's house that he wanted and needed to be with Alex forever. He walked slowly to his room, trying to think of how to go about asking her to marry him.

The days before Christmas flew by for George as he showed Alex around the area, introducing her to anyone and everyone they came across. He took her horseback riding several times, each time to a different place from his childhood. He took pictures of her to help him capture the time they spent together, wanting to preserve it forever. They spent time with his family, letting the love that family members had for each other reach out and encompass her. Each day he came to love her more, but as much as he wanted to propose to her, something always held him back. He would plan out a day's activities and decide when and where he would propose, but when the time came, the words stuck in his throat. He prayed day and night that he would know when the time was right, but he didn't feel like he was getting an answer. He picked up his journal that he felt compelled to bring with him, and skimmed through it until he came to the entries he was looking for.

June 3
Today we met with a new family. Scott and Mary have three children, ages four, six, and nine. Although Scott is receptive, Mary seems to have had a bad experience with religion as a child, and doesn't want to listen to the discussions anymore. Scott has accepted the challenge to read the Book of Mormon and is excited to learn more about the church. The nine year-old, John, is interested, too, but if Mary is vocal about her dislike, we don't know what will happen with him.

June 4
We met with Scott and John again. Scott is already well into First Nephi and he's been telling John the stories as he's gone along. They both have prayed about it and want to be baptized. We have all decided to set up a fast for Mary. She's adamant that John will not be baptized. We're going to fast tomorrow, Thursday, and Saturday for her. We're to meet with Scott and John on those days and go over more of the discussions with them.

June 8,
We have fasted three days this week and I don't feel like we're closer to our goal. Mary is still insistent that John not be baptized, and is almost to the point of asking us to not come back. We were able to talk to Scott by himself for a few minutes and suggested that he and John not talk with Mary about it, but keep praying that her heart will soften. We will continue to pray for her as well.

June 30

It's been almost a month now and Mary is still not happy with us. She has gone from being hostile to a quiet, although grudging, acceptance of Scott's joining the church. His baptism is scheduled for next Sunday. We're hoping that Scott's joining the church, and his example, will help her to come around. We have continued to pray for her, but I still don't feel like I've had an answer. I know that things happen in the Lord's time, but I'm worried about the effect this will have on John.

August 4

I am so grateful for the Lord's understanding of things. Whenever we have gone over to visit with Scott and John, Mary has taken the younger children to another room and hardly said a word to us. This morning she called us up and very humbly asked us over for dinner. When we got there, we found that she had prepared one of the best dinners I have ever had. While we ate, Mary was quiet but very cordial. After dinner we went into the living room with Scott, Mary, and John. Mary looked us both in the eyes, then quietly started to cry.

"I am so sorry for the way I've treated you boys. I am very ashamed of my behavior and I hope you'll forgive me."

We quickly assured her that we held no hard feelings towards her, that we understood that not everyone was going to react the way we'd like them to when family and friends joined the church.

"Thank you. I feel better. I would like John to be baptized if he still wants to. I would also like to be baptized. I feel that I should tell you what has changed my mind about the church.

"I have felt horrible about the way I've been feeling and treating all of you. Scott, my dear husband, I swore to honor you when we married. I have not felt like I have been doing that. I have seen myself snapping at the children and picking fights with you, and I haven't liked it. I felt so bad that the other night. I couldn't sleep because I kept thinking of thing things I'd said and done. I knelt down next to my bed and prayed that the bad feeling in my heart would go away. After I finished my prayer, I got back into bed and was able to sleep. Today I got the feeling that I should call my mother. Even though I had talked with her last week, I called her. I talked with her about my own experiences with going to

89

church and we were able to get a lot of things out in the open and worked out. I still had some negative feelings, so I decided to pray some more. As I prayed I felt like I should get Scott's Book of Mormon and open it up to 3 Nephi 11:29. It was like someone had whispered the reference in my ear, so I had no doubt that I was supposed to read that verse. When I read it, I knew what had happened. Satan had entered my heart and had stirred me up to anger. After reading that scripture I knelt down and prayed again. This time I prayed to know if what you were trying to teach me was true. I felt a warmth spread all over me and a pair of arms encircle me, giving me a hug that I had long denied that I needed, the hug of a long-lost friend. I know now that the Church is true, and I want to be baptized as soon as possible."

All of us sat there in stunned silence as we listened to her story, and I knew in my heart that our prayers had been answered. I am so glad that Heavenly Father is in charge. Otherwise I would have missed out on this wonderful experience, as would Scott, Mary, and John.

Scott and Mary were both crying openly and hugging each other when I finally had the presence of mind to talk again. Even then I was choked up with the feeling of the Spirit that was so strong in the room.

"We'll be glad to help you to get ready for your baptism, Mary. Shall we go over the next discussion, or come back tomorrow?"

Mary said that there was no time like the present, so we ended a wonderful evening with a discussion and a heartfelt prayer of thanks from Scott.

I hope I never forget that all things happen in the Lord's time and way.

When he had finished reading, George put the journal away and knelt down in prayer. He prayed that he would have the patience he needed until the time was right to talk with Alex about getting married. He prayed that he would be able to continue to help her on her journey, and that he would be mindful of the changes she was going through. With a sense of peace, he ended the prayer and got up to go find her.

After looking over the whole house, he found Alex in Starlight's stall, talking softly as she brushed the horse down.

George slowed as he came close enough to understand what she was. He knew that he shouldn't eavesdrop, but at the same time he wanted to know what she was saying to the horse.

"—and he's so sweet. He's taking the time to make sure I'm having a good time, and he sees to it that I'm almost always laughing. And when I'm not laughing, he's helping me to feel better about things that happened to me when I was young. I've never met anyone who has so genuinely cared about someone else. Of course I've had friends, but none of them seemed to care about me more than they cared about themselves.

"And he's so cute. There's a look he gets every now and then that makes my breath catch and makes my stomach feel funny. Sometimes I would like—who's there?"

"It's me," George said, walking over to the stall.

Starlight stuck her head over the door and shoved his shoulder as he walked up to them.

"Sorry, girl. I don't have anything with me this time," he told the horse as he petted her blaze.

"How long have you been standing there?" Alex asked.

Going into the stall, he took the brush from her hand and set it on a small ledge.

"Long enough to want to do this," he said, taking her into his arms and giving her a long hug. "I think you're pretty cute, too."

She pulled away enough to look at him.

"To quote Brother Carmichael, 'Are you two young-uns dating?'" she asked, her eyebrow quirked.

"I'd like to date you, Alex. In the short time I've known you, you've helped me to have a deeper understanding of love. I know it's fast, but I love you."

The minute he said it, he knew it was the right time to tell her. No matter what her reaction, he knew that he had to tell her how he felt.

Alex froze for a few seconds, a look of pure terror in her eyes before she blinked it away. She took a deep breath and seemed to brace herself.

"I—I care about you a lot, too."

George took heart and gave her a brief, hard hug before letting her go. He could tell the amount of courage it took her to say that. It wasn't exactly what he would have liked to hear, but he knew it was a step in the right direction.

"You looked scared for a second there. Do you feel like talking about it?" he asked quietly.

"I don't think I'm quite ready to talk about it yet," she said slowly. "I think I will be soon, though. I just need to work through a few things first."

"Whenever you're ready, I'm here to listen."

"I know. Thank you. It really means a lot to me."

That Sunday was Christmas Eve, and Alex joined them at church. George was glad to see that she joined in the singing and listened attentively to the talks and lessons. The light in her eyes seemed to get brighter and brighter, and he could sense a peace and calm in her that hadn't been there before. Between each meeting, more and more people who had met her stopped to say hi and to say they were glad to see her. Sister Carmichael talked with her alone for a few minutes before the older lady walked away with a big smile on her face.

"What did you tell her? She's smiling bright enough to rival the sun."

"I told her that we were dating. She seems to approve."

George chuckled and shook his head, but didn't comment.

After the Sacrament had been passed his family sang the song they had spent the better part of the month practicing. The Spirit was strong by the end of the song, and George noticed Alex surreptitiously wiping away tears from her eyes. Without looking at her, he pulled a handkerchief from his breast pocket and handed it to her.

"Thank you," she whispered.

"You're welcome," he whispered back.

After the Sacrament Meeting was over, George guided Alex to a quiet spot and asked her if it was all right to have the missionaries come over to talk with her before she left for California.

"I would like that," she said. "I feel more at home here at your church than I have in any other church. I'd like to have that feeling with me all the time, not just here."

"I see the sister missionaries right now. Let's go ask them if they have time to come over today or tomorrow."

As they walked over to the missionaries, George took Alex's hand. When she didn't pull away, he rewarded her hand with a squeeze.

"Hi, Sister Tan, Sister Tatafu. How are you today?" George asked them.

"We're well, Brother Hart. How about you and your parents? Their musical number was very good," Sister Tatafu said.

"Thank you, I'll tell them you said so. We are doing very well, thank you. Have you met Alex?"

"No, we haven't," Sister Tan said, her Asian accent very pronounced.

George made the introductions before making his request.

"Alex would like to learn more about the church. Would you be able to come over, either tonight or tomorrow? She'll be leaving for California on Tuesday night, and we wanted to have you visit with us once before she left."

Sister Tatafu pulled out their calendar. After a minute she looked up smiling.

"Yes, I do think we can squeeze you in. How would tonight at six be for you?"

"That would be perfect," Alex said. "I'm so glad that you have time to stop by."

"Not a problem," Sister Tan said. "This is what we are here for. We have an appointment we need to get to now, so we'd better go. We'll see you tonight then."

Chapter 7

At dinner that evening Alex listened to the chatter as everyone talked about what they had heard and gained from the lessons.

"Our lesson in Primary was about tithing," Cherish said. "It's amazing to see these six- and seven-year-olds so excited to pay tithing. When I asked if they knew why we paid tithing, Suzie McCall said the reason was because we 'ought to give something, and my big sister says that is an easy number to figure out'."

"Of course her sister said that," Jane said, laughing. "I helped her with her math three weeks ago when I baby-sat her, and that was the only multiplication that she understood already. It took all night for her to get the other numbers figured out."

As Alex helped herself to more corn, she asked thoughtfully, "Why do churches want a us to donate money, is it just to pay the leaders a salary? I don't remember ever being taught why, just 'because you're supposed to'."

Kurt answered in a voice that George had only heard when the Spirit was guiding him. "The Lord has given us everything that we have, from our very lives, to the air we breathe, to the planet we live on. Out of everything He's given us, he has asked us to give back only one-tenth of what we ourselves earn. This money doesn't go to make the people who run His church rich or lazy, it goes to help build His kingdom here on earth. It goes to help those who are less fortunate than we are by providing them food and clothing. It also goes to build meetinghouses and temples. It helps the leaders of the Church and the missionaries to fulfill their callings to travel throughout the world, sharing their message of love and peace. Sharing the message that the Christ lives and loves us, and that through him, all can be saved in the kingdom of His Father, our Heavenly Father. I've been on a mission, I've seen firsthand what blessings come from dedicating your life to serving those around you, sharing the message that the Lord would have us share. I have seen what blessings come from paying a full and faithful tithe. Those who give to impress others or who give out of habit, give in vain; but those who give because they care, because they want to show their thanks to Heavenly Father, will have the blessings that come from doing so. I know that giving back a tenth of what I have will never repay the debt I owe my Savior, who gave up His very life so that I might live again, not just with God, but with my *Father* in Heaven."

Everyone was quiet for the rest of the meal, giving Alex the opportunity to ponder what had been said. George carefully examined her face to see what he might glean from its smooth lines. Her forehead creased slightly as she absorbed what Kurt had told her.

After dinner, Jane and Kurt said they still had presents to wrap.

At six the sister missionaries arrived.

"Sister Tan, Sister Tatafu, how are you tonight?" George asked.

"We are well," Sister Tan said in her Asian accent. "And how are you and Alex?"

"We are well also," Alex answered.

They all sat down in the living room.

"We'd like to start with a prayer, if that's all right with you?" Sister Tatafu asked.

"Certainly," George said.

He asked Sister Tan if she would offer the prayer. Sister Tan prayed that the Spirit would be present and that Alex would get the answers she was looking for.

Sister Tan and Sister Tatafu spent the next fifteen minutes going over the basics of the gospel. Alex asked questions from time to time, but mostly she just listened. George said the closing prayer. Before the sisters left, Sister Tan gave Alex a Book of Mormon and challenged her to read it and pray to know if it were true.

"Thank you, I will," Alex said, taking the book of scripture.

They saw the sisters to the door and thanked them again for coming. Once they had left George asked if Alex wanted to help him with the last few presents he had to wrap.

"Maybe for a little bit. I'm feeling kind of restless tonight."

"That's okay. If you want, you can go snowshoeing or take a walk," he suggested.

"That sounds like a good idea, I think I will take a walk in a few minutes," she said thoughtfully.

They went into his room to wrap presents. As Alex hadn't seen the room of his youth before, he let her wander around and look.

She picked up a 4-H trophy for raising sheep, and another one for raising rabbits.

"I've never heard of 4-H. What is it?"

"It's kind of like FFA, Future Farmers of America, except it's not school-sponsored. It's mostly a summer program for kids in farming areas. For those who are raising livestock it can be a year round project."

"Did you like growing up here on a ranch? I mean, the closest I've ever come to 'raising' an animal was taking care of my cat. When I was at summer camp one year we had to help take care of the horses, but the staff did most of it."

"I did for the most part. So many kids grow up not knowing who their neighbors are, trusting no one but their parents, teachers, and a few friends. Here, we leave our doors unlocked unless we go out of town, and if we don't know someone, it's because they're new to the area. The part I didn't like so much was that if I got into trouble in school, by word of mouth my parents most likely found out before I got home and were waiting for me. You have your organized neighborhood watch in the city; here we do it on our own, just because we know who should be where and when.

"One time some kids did some minor vandalism to one of the teacher's home. Someone saw it happen and told my teacher, and the teacher told all the kids in her classes that she wouldn't press charges if the culprits came forward. I guess they did, because we never heard of anyone getting into trouble about it," he told Alex.

"Wow! That would blow some people's minds, caring that much for one another. My block tried to get a neighborhood watch going, but no one wanted to take responsibility for running it or helping out. Everyone had a reason for not being 'able' to help," she said.

As they talked, George pulled a shopping bag out of his closet. The bag held the presents he wanted to wrap as well as some paper and tape. He gestured for Alex to join him on the floor, and handed her a few presents and a roll of wrapping paper.

They talked about some of the differences in growing up in the city versus growing up in the country as they wrapped the presents in bright holiday paper. It only took them ten minutes to wrap the presents and return them to the shopping bag, to be put under the tree later.

"Would you like me to come with you, or would you rather go on your walk by yourself?" George asked as they left his room.

"I'd like to go by myself, I think," Alex said.

"Do you know how long you plan to be gone? I wouldn't want you to go wandering off and get lost and no one know you were missing until morning," he said, smiling.

"I'm not sure, but probably only about ten minutes or so. I've noticed it gets right chilly here at night," she said, smiling back.

"Then I recommend that after you leave the front yard you turn right and go down until you get to a group of tree stumps, and then head back. That's about a ten to fifteen minute walk, depending on how fast you're walking."

"Thanks. I'll be back soon."

"Oh, just a heads-up. Jane will mostly likely wake you up so early that you'll want to kill her. Just ignore her and get up when you're ready. We won't start without you."

97

"Not start without… You mean…? I haven't gotten any of you anything! I didn't even think about it with all that's been going on. Great! Now I feel bad. Here I've been staying with all of you and didn't think to get even a token present for your mom and dad," she said, looking crestfallen.

"Alex, don't worry about it," he said gently. "None of us expected you to get us anything. Your present to us has been your being here with us this past week. I told you, we're used to having extra bodies around, and since Doug and I have moved out, it's quieter than what my folks are used to."

"If you say so, I'm not sure I believe you, though."

"Sweetheart, think about my parents. Do you really think they would hold something like this against you?"

"No, I guess not."

George stood leaning against the doorframe as Alex walked away. He was still surprised at how fast everything had happened, but it still felt right. He retrieved his bag of presents, added the ones for Alex, and went to put them under the tree.

In the living room Cherish was already putting a few presents under the tree. She looked up as he came into view and smiled.

"How are you doing, honey? It's been kind of busy the last week or so," she said.

"I'm well. It has been busy, but in the best possible way," he said, thoughtfully.

"Are you sure you're okay? You sound like you're trying to work something out," she said.

"No. I'm okay, just marveling at how the Lord shows us His hand in things."

"You mean Alex? Yes, she is a dear, isn't she?" Cherish said, smiling with the wisdom of experience. "Have you told her you love her yet?"

Startled by the question, George just stared at his mother.

"Oh, don't deny it. Everyone can tell you care about her," she told him.

Smiling sheepishly he said, "Yes, I have. And before you ask, I prayed about it already, as well. I know not to make a decision this important without the Lord's help."

Smiling proudly she responded, "That's my boy. As much as I'd like to see you sealed in the temple, the Lord knows best. If He says it's okay to proceed, then who am I to say nay?"

George put the bag down and went to give Cherish a hug.

"Thank you, Mom. It means a lot to me that you're okay with this. Now, what did you get me?"

He pretended to root through the packages for a minute until she scolded him. He laughed and started to put his presents under the tree.

Shortly after Alex came back in from her walk, the bell for scriptures rang out and a everyone was assembled in the living room with their scriptures. Kurt asked Jane to offer the opening prayer, and then they took turns reading. The Spirit was strong in the room as they read about the birth of the Savior and the people who came to pay homage to Him.

After the closing prayer, Alex commented, "You know, I've never thought about it before, but Christ was born in the stables. He had what was probably the humblest of beginnings, but He is the King of All, and He didn't let how He came into the world affect His mission. He knew that He could overcome anything, even death. I wonder what that kind of knowledge would do for someone?"

"Alex, we *do* have that kind of knowledge," Jane said earnestly. "The whole point of Christ's coming was to make a way for the rest of us, imperfections and all, to get back to our Father. By His being perfect, He showed us the way to live. When we fail, His suffering on the cross allows Him to tell Heavenly Father 'they did the best they could with the knowledge they had. I have paid the price for their failings. Let them in'. When we die, it's only for a while. In the end, Christ will come again, and those who have died will be resurrected like He was, and our bodies will be perfect.

"So we have the knowledge that we will overcome death. But we still need to do our best to follow His example before we join Him and our Father in Heaven."

Understanding flooded into Alex as she listened to Jane, and everyone realized that this had been missing from Alex's life.

"Thank you," Alex said simply. "I'm going to go to my room to think. Goodnight everyone."

Each echoed her goodnight and watched as she left.

Once she was out of earshot, Jane piped up, "You'd better get her while you can. Once she gets it figured out, you'll be left in the dust of all the other guys who'll be after her."

George scowled at her.

"I'm working on it, okay? I love her and plan on asking her to marry me as soon as I feel the time is right. Right now I'm trying to help her get the answers she needs. Does that take care of your concerns?" he asked.

"O. K., got it," Jane said, raising her hands defensively.

"I'm sorry, Jane. It's just that I am working on it and you're not the first person in the last five hours to ask me about that. It's hard enough for me not to just ask her, but I feel that she needs to do some healing first."

"I understand. I'll try to mind my own business, but let me know if you need to talk, all right?"

"Will do. I'm going to the darkroom for a bit."

In the darkroom he took one of his favorite pictures of Alex and proceeded to enlarge it, trying various techniques to change the look and feel of it. After about two hours he had what he wanted and was satisfied with his work. On his way to bed, he stopped in the living room briefly.

Chapter 8

CLANK-CLANG-CLANK! CLANG-A-LANG!

George woke with a groan. He didn't have to look at the clock to know what time it was, or to think what day it was. Christmas morning at this parents' meant that at 6:00 a.m. Jane would make enough noise to wake the dead (or those who at that moment wished they were dead).

"Merry Christmas! Merry Christmas!" Jane's yell came muffled though the closed door and the pillow over his head, but could still be understood.

CLANK-CLANG-CLANK!

George knew that the only way to get any more sleep was to go to Jane, so he threw off the covers and rushed to the door. The banging and clanging got louder as he opened the door and started to run.

He found Jane in the front hall, fully dressed, banging away on an old cowbell with a wooden spoon.

Covering his ears and yelling to be heard over the noise, he shouted, "Jane! Please stop! Alex isn't used to this."

Jane stopped banging on his last word, so his voice was heard loud and clear.

"Gee-whiz, George! You don't have to yell," she said, dropping the cowbell and spoon to cover her ears. She was smiling.

"Uh, yeah, I do, to be heard over the din you're making. Have some respect for us old fogies who want to sleep, okay?"

"Nope, old fogey or not, you know the routine. Anyway, got you up, didn't it?" she said smugly.

"It might have, but I'm going back to bed. I told Alex to stay in bed as long as she wanted."

"I guess she wanted to get up then," Jane said, pointing behind him.

Turning around, George saw a sleepy-eyed Alex in bunny slippers and fuzzy powder pink robe coming down the hall.

"You said she might try to wake me up, George, not raise the dead," Alex said around a yawn.

"I also said you didn't have to get up," he told her.

"Well, I'm up now and I don't think I'll be able to go back to sleep. Where are your parents? I'd've thought they'd be here by now, too."

"This is the one morning Dad doesn't have to get up to feed the animals because I do it, so he and Mom are still in bed. They decided that semi-soundproofing their room would be a good idea years ago, so they might not have actually heard anything," Jane told her.

Alex chuckled. "I don't blame them," she said. "Since we're up, what's the plan?"

"We get whatever's in our stockings and then we have to eat breakfast. At that point we goof around until Mom and Dad get up. We learned a long time ago that if we try to get them up sooner, they take even longer, on purpose," Jane said.

They went into the living room and Alex gasped at what she saw. Even Jane paused for a second. All the lights were out except the ones on the tree. Presents spilled out from under the tree, but what had stopped them was the picture of Alex carefully balanced in the tree's branches.

The 12x10 picture was a close-up of Alex the day they had gone to Sun Valley. George had cropped Jane and Nancy out of the picture and focused entirely on the joy on Alex's face. He had blurred the focus a little, giving the print a dreamlike quality.

After a few seconds Alex looked at George in perplexed wonder.

"Do you like it?" he asked somewhat nervously.

"Like it? I—I can't begin to tell you how much I love it. No one but my parents has ever done anything so wonderful for me. Thank you so much."

With tears in her eyes, she flung herself at him. He had just enough time to brace himself for her embrace. He held her until she released him. Then he reluctantly let her go.

"I thought you might like a reminder of your time here, and that this would be a good one. If you like, I can give you a copy of the whole picture and some of the others that Jane and I took. I'm glad you like it," he told her, wiping the tears off one of her cheeks.

"Hey, you two are under the mistletoe," Jane said, bringing them back to a reality.

They looked up and saw that they were indeed under the famous vegetation.

Shrugging, Alex said, "Tradition is tradition."

With a smile George complied, bending down to kiss her lightly on the lips. As he pulled back, it was all he could do not to propose right then. As the words were forming, he heard in his mind, as though someone were speaking directly to him, "Not yet, have patience." Despite his disappointment that the time to propose to Alex had not yet come, he was comforted by the instructions. They were proof that the time would come when he would be able to ask the question that burned in his heart.

George cleared his throat and looked around, trying to think of something to say to break the tension. Looking over at Jane, he saw her grinning at him, her stocking in hand.

"Stockings. Let's look in our stockings," he said with some desperation.

"What? Oh, uh, sure," Alex said, "Would I even have a stocking?"

Jane took pity on George and answered, "Yes. Mom always has three or four extra ones just in case. Over here, this one's yours. Look. Mom even put your name on it."

Jane held out a candy-cane-striped felt stocking that had 'ALEX' written on it in green felt letters dusted with gold glitter. It was stuffed with goodies. Alex tried surreptitiously to wipe away more tears.

George went and got his stocking from the sofa where the others had been. Jane and George sat on the floor next to the coffee table and started to empty their respective stockings like it was the first time either had done so.

"Oh, look, I got a hacky-sack!" Jane said.

"And I got a Rudolph Pez dispenser with orange Pez. That completes my collection of Christmas characters!" George told Jane.

"Ugh! Walnuts," Jane lamented.

"I'll trade you my hazelnuts for your walnuts," George offered.

"Deal!" Jane said, handing over the offending nuts.

Not looking up from sorting out his hazelnuts, George asked Alex if she was going to join them.

"I will in a bit. I want to watch you two for a minute. It's been a long time since I've seen this kind of interaction over stockings and I want to savor it."

"Your choice," Jane said, "but it's more fun if you join in."

Jane and George continued to swap items and comment on what they had gotten. A minute or two later Alex sat down and dumped out her loot, too. In another minute she had joined in the haggling to get what she liked and to trade what she didn't.

Half an hour later, after quick breakfasts of cold cereal, they were back at the coffee table playing with the cheap toys from their stockings. George was trying to run over Jane's pocket-sized doll with his Hot Wheels car, and Alex's miniature T-rex was trying to eat both car and doll, when Cherish and Kurt walked in, both still in their night clothes and robes.

"I see it didn't take you long to join in their mischief," Kurt said to Alex.

Alex looked up, slightly startled, than grinned.

"No, sir, it didn't. Hard not to with these two as examples."

Kurt chuckled as he and Cherish walked hand-in-hand over to them.

Everyone quickly knelt down. By now Alex recognized the signs that meant a prayer was going to be said, so she followed suit. After Cherish gave heartfelt thanks for all their blessings and the opportunity to focus on the birth of the Savior, the group got down to the business of presents. Once George had distributed the presents, setting aside the ones for Doug and Nancy, they took turns opening them, starting with Alex, since she was the guest. Jane took pictures the entire time.

Alex was very excited by the number of presents she had been given, and once again expressed her regret for not getting them anything. Cherish and Kurt waved away her concerns, stating as George had that just having her there was present enough. Finally satisfied, she started to open her presents. Jane had given her a funky pair of earrings and a couple hair clips "for when you feel like expressing your inner child". Cherish had given Alex a beginner's cookbook with her phone number written in it, in case Alex ever needed help with a recipe. Kurt had carved a small bear for her. After Alex had opened and admired each gift, she gave each of them a hug to show her appreciation.

"These are wonderful, thank you all. This has been one of the best Christmases," she told everyone.

"Oh, look. I think I missed a couple of presents under the tree," George said, smiling.

He went over and pulled out the two presents he had hidden in the back. He brought them over to Alex and kissed her on the cheek.

"Merry Christmas. And Alex, may all your dreams come true," he said.

Blushing slightly at the kiss, Alex took the two small boxes and carefully opened the first one. It was the music box from the gift shop. Alex twisted the wind-up crank a couple times, and the sweet music of Für Elise filled the air. Alex gave George a tear-filled look of gratitude.

"I don't remember the last time I cried so much," she said, half joking, as she wiped them way.

"It's okay," he told her. "Happy tears are good tears. Open up the other one."

She followed his instructions and was soon gazing at the beautiful glass figurine inside the second box. She carefully lifted out the hummingbird on the morning glory vine so everyone could see it.

"I will find a place for them, even if I have to get rid of my microwave," she told George when she finally looked up.

He gently took both gifts and set them on the coffee table. He then sat down next to her and gave her a hug. Alex hugged him hard for a few seconds and then pulled away.

"I love you," she said simply before hugging him again.

George hugged her hard and grinned. Yes, it had been worth the wait to hear her say those words. Very much worth the wait.

Kurt cleared his throat to remind them they had an audience. Alex pulled away, embarrassed at being caught declaring feelings.

"I'm sorry. I forgot that we weren't alone," she said.

"That's perfectly fine, dear," Cherish said. "We've been wondering how long it would take and now we don't have to wait any longer. Now this might be jumping the gun a bit, and we know that declaring your love does not a wedding guarantee, but for what it's worth, we would be delighted to have you in the family."

Alex and George looked at each other and then burst out laughing.

"Yes, Cherish, it is jumping the gun a bit, but thank you for your candor. If we get to that point, I would love to be part of your family," Alex said, smiling. "Even if we don't get married, I'd like to stay in touch. You all have been so wonderful and welcoming."

"As far as Kurt and I are concerned, you are always welcome. Consider yourself adopted."

Nodding, Alex said, "I will. Mom."

Cherish smiled with satisfaction.

Jane was the next to open her presents. Kurt and Cherish had given her a gift card to her favorite clothing store at the mall, a bottle of bubble bath, and some bath salts. George had given her a book she had been looking at when they were at the mall, and a CD by a group she liked. She gave them all hugs and voiced her approval on everything.

Kurt had Cherish open the gift he had gotten for her. The box was small and square and about the size of a wallet, about two inches deep. After carefully removing the tissue paper, Cherish discovered a necklace in white gold. The pendant was a cluster of small diamonds held up by the hands of two stylized figures whose bent knees touched, forming a circle. Kurt took the necklace from Cherish's shaking fingers and opened the clasp. She moved so he could put it around her neck.

"Dearheart, this is to show how much I appreciate all you do to help me. Our family, the farming and ranching, I would never have done so well without you right next to me, cheering me on. I know that I don't tell you very often that I love you, but I do, with all my heart."

George had never seen his father do something this romantic, and he was glad that his dad had decided to do it in front of them. He could tell by the look on Cherish's face that this gesture meant a lot to her, too. She hugged her husband, and this time she was the one crying.

"You have always been the best husband to me. I've never wanted to be with anyone else since we met. You help me so much. I love you, too."

The other three found something else to look at while the two kissed. Once Cherish had composed herself, they finished up the presents. Jane and George had pitched in to get their parents a set of books about the modern-day prophets, and Cherish had given Kurt a new pair of work gloves and boots and a new electric razor.

Nancy and Doug came over at nine, and once again there were presents. Nancy gave Cherish a box that looked like it might contain a watch or bracelet, and asked her to open it first. Cherish opened it and pulled out a folded piece of paper.

"Read it out loud," Nancy directed.

With a puzzled look on her face, Cherish did as she was instructed.

"We're pregnant," she read. "We're…?"

Cherish looked sharply at the couple and in a very un-Cherish like way shouted, "You're pregnant?!" She then went to hug Nancy and Doug. "When did you find out?"

Laughing, Nancy said, "About two days ago. It was hard not to say anything about it, but thought it would make a good present today."

"It sure does," Jane said. "Oh my gosh! I'm going to be an aunt! I'm going to be an aunt!!"

"Yes, you are, Squirt," Doug said, smiling from ear to ear.

"When are you due?" Alex put in.

"I'm not sure yet. I'll set up an appointment tomorrow to go in and find out. Turns out that's why I wasn't feeling well the other day."

"That will do it," Cherish said, nodding.

"Congratulations. Maybe now you'll understand what your mother went through when you were little, Doug. Not that I don't think there'll be anything you can't handle," Kurt said quickly, noticing Nancy's raised eyebrow. "Just that he was something of a stinker before he learned to behave."

Everyone but Doug laughed at that.

The next hour was spent opening the rest of the presents, checking out one another's gifts, and in general holiday cheer.

Once things calmed down, Alex went to start packing for her flight back to Tahoe, and George went to work on a going-away present for her. He spent a couple of hours working on it in the darkroom and in his dad's office. Alex tried to join him, but George had already asked Jane to run interference by inviting Alex to join her for one last horseback ride before she had to leave.

Dinner that night was a big affair with the whole family. Cherish cooked the turkey and rolls, Jane the mashed potatoes, yams, and gravy, Nancy the green bean casserole and cranberry sauce. Alex helped make the apple and pumpkin pies under Cherish's watchful eye. Doug and George tried to sneak in for nibbles, but after being caught twice, decided there were too many cooks in the kitchen to get away with it. They decided to play a game of Risk with Kurt instead.

The game was almost over when the dinner bell rang, much to Doug's relief as he was about to lose his last two countries to Kurt.

"Saved by the bell," Doug said, starting to put away the game pieces.

"Tell you what, boys, my ribs are about ready to poke outta my skin I'm so hungry. Your mother said if I was going to eat as much as I planned to, I'd have to have a light lunch. All I had was a ham sandwich and glass of cider. Good job, by the way. One of the best batches you've ever made, George," Kurt said.

"Thanks, Dad. My stomach's about ready to start growling, too. I haven't had much aside from the stuff from my stocking. My fault, I know, but doesn't make me any less hungry," George said, his stomach grumbling as if on cue.

All three men laughed as they put the last few pieces of the game away and headed to the kitchen.

After everyone was seated and the food blessed, organized chaos erupted as everyone filled their plates. Once everyone settled into eating, George, Doug, and Jane started to regale Nancy and Alex with tales of Christmases past. Jane told about the Christmas when she was eight when Doug and George had sneaked into her room and put a rubber snake on her pillow. When Jane woke up the next morning, even Kurt and Cherish heard her scream through their partially soundproofed room. As punishment, the boys had to wait until the next day to open their presents.

Doug next told about the Christmas when George got his first razor and shaving cream.

"George thought it would be funny to put shaving cream in my hand that night and then tickle my nose to try to get me to swipe at the tickle. What he didn't realize, though, was that the sound of the shaving cream coming out of the can woke me up enough to figure out what was happening, and I smeared the shaving cream all over his face instead," Doug said proudly.

This went on until Cherish, even though she was chuckling at the escapades herself, called a halt to it. The rest of the meal was fairly silent as the food settled.

Doug pushed his plate away after finishing off his third serving of potatoes and gravy.

"Oh, that was good. Thank you, ladies, for cooking the food. I think the food coma is starting to kick in, though. I'm going to lie down on the couch for a bit," he said.

"Oh, no you don't. You know the rule," Cherish said. "We cook it, you help clean up. We took care of most of it; you boys just need to put the leftovers away. You don't have to worry about the turkey pan this year since I used an oven bag, but all the other pots and pans need to be washed before the food dries in them."

109

George felt like arguing to get out of doing kitchen duty, but he knew he would be wasting his breath. Cherish usually didn't mind washing up after cooking, but on holidays or special occasions when a lot of food had been cooked, the men got to put the leftovers away and do the dishes. He got up and started to collect the plates and silverware. Doug followed by getting the glasses. Kurt, by virtue of being the head of the house, got to sit back and let the boys do most of the work, although he did help out by getting the containers for the leftovers.

Jane, Nancy, Cherish, and Alex went into the living room and put on *It's a Wonderful Life*. About halfway through the movie, after the food was all put away and the dishes done, Doug and George joined them. Kurt had to get up early the next morning to check on some of the fences, so he had already gone to bed.

After the movie was over, they served the pie. Everyone agreed that Alex had done a great job. Alex smiled at the compliments, but gave credit where credit was due.

"It was all Cherish," she said. "I just did what she told me to do. I'll take the compliments more seriously when I do the whole thing by myself and it still turns out edible."

"I don't think you have anything to worry about, dear," Cherish said. "Now that you've tried a few things with help, I think you'll be fine on your own. Sometimes we just need someone to go over the basics with us until we can do it ourselves."

After dessert, everyone went to bed. George said his prayers and then wrote in his journal about the day's events, pausing over his recounting of Alex's declaration of love. He still felt he needed to wait a bit before proposing, but he was happy that she was finally able to admit her feelings for him.

The next morning George awoke to a knock on his door. Groggily, he got up to answer it. He found Alex there, dressed, holding a glass of orange juice.

"Good morning," she said as she handed him the juice. "I thought I'd come get you out of bed this morning."

He smiled as he took the proffered glass.

"Thank you. I hope you got permission from Mom, though. We still aren't allowed to have food outside the kitchen, except for when we're watching a movie."

"Yes, she said it was okay."

He drank half the glass before stepping out of the doorway to head towards the kitchen. As he got closer, the smell of bacon almost had him floating. He inhaled deeply.

"Mmm, smells good. Are you cooking it, or is Mom? Doesn't matter, smells wonderful," he said. "What's for breakfast?"

"Your mom showed me how to make Eggs Benedict this morning. With a side of bacon."

He stopped her just outside the kitchen and gave her a quick kiss.

"I do believe you are trying to woo me with your cooking," he teased.

"A man cannot live on love alone, as much as he might want to, and if we do stay together, I don't want you dying because I killed you with my cooking," she said, smiling back at him.

After breakfast George finished getting ready for the day. While he took a shower, Alex finished up her packing. Once everything was ready to be put in the jeep, they still had some time left, so they took turns playing songs on the piano and singing. Jane joined them partway through.

Once it was time to leave for the airport and her things were packed into the jeep, Alex said good-bye to everyone.

"Make sure you call if you need help with any cooking," Cherish said, giving Alex a hug.

"I will. Thank you for the help."

"Don't work too hard. Remember to laugh once in a while," Jane told her.

"I'll watch one comedy a week," Alex said, smiling at the younger woman.

"Keep in touch. We really enjoyed having you around," Kurt said, offering her his hand.

"I will. You guys are more family to me already than my family has been for a long time."

Jane handed her a present.

"Jane, you didn't have to give me anything," Alex said plaintively.

"This is mostly George's, but from all of us, too," Jane said.

Alex opened the small flat package and found a photo album with the pictures George had promised. George watched as Alex flipped through it and saw the pictures of the trip to Sun Valley and some of the family throughout the years. He watched as Alex blinked away the tears then hugged each of them.

"This has been the best Christmas ever," Alex told them.

George looked at his watch.

"We need to get going, Alex," he said, all but dragged Alex to the jeep.

Once inside, they settled in for the long drive.

"Would you like to listen to some music?" he asked.

"Not right now, thank you."

They drove in silence for most of the way to the airport. George had learned that silence was needed at times and was not something to fear, so he left Alex to her thoughts.

As they came into Boise proper, Alex asked, "How are we going to do a long-distance relationship? I think we both forgot that we weren't going to be at your parents' forever."

"Good question. I'm willing to drive up once or twice a month, and there's always the phone and email. Maybe we can get web cams. If you want something badly enough, there's very little that will stop you, Mom says."

"From what I've seen, Cherish is probably seldom wrong. Maybe we can take turns going back and forth. It might be hard, but sometimes having space built in is good, too."

"I need to get gas really quick. If you want to grab something for the plane, you can do that, too," he offered.

"That would be good. Prices at airports are usually higher anyway."

While George pumped the gas, Alex went inside the convenience store and bought some things to eat on the plane. Once back on the road, it was only a short drive to the airport. In the drop-off area George got out to help unload Alex's luggage. Then he gave her a long hug.

When she finally pulled away, she said, "I'd better get going. I'll call you when I get in. I'm going to miss you."

"I'm going to miss you, too. Stay safe. I'll look forward to your call. Tell Mrs. H. hi for me, and thanks for sending you. I love you," he said as he brushed her hair over her ear.

"I love you, too. I better go now."

Reluctantly she picked up her bags and suitcase and turned around. George watched her go, feeling like a large piece of him was being torn out with every step she took. The only thing that stopped him from going after her was the knowledge that he would see her again in a few weeks.

He drove home in a melancholy state, listening to his favorite music to try to help him feel better. For once, it didn't work.

Chapter 9

Over the next couple of days George tried to get over his feeling of loss by keeping busy. He didn't think he fooled anyone, but he tried to keep what he was feeling to himself. He visited some of the people from church, including the Carmichaels, but that didn't work since everyone asked about Alex. He told them that she had left, but that they were going to keep in touch. He had to tell the Carmichaels a bit more of what had happened.

"You look like you're not doing so well, George," Brother Carmichael said. "Are you okay?"

George smiled sadly. "No, I'm not. Alex has been gone for less than seventy-two hours and even though we talk every night, I feel like I've lost my best friend. I miss having her around, seeing her smile. I know I'm going to see her again once I get back to California, but that feels like forever right now. I'm hoping once we're at least in the same state, it'll be better. But until we're together again, I'm thinking that I'm going to keep feeling like this."

Brother and Sister Carmichael looked at one another, then at George, and smiled.

"I don't know about you, but for us it didn't get any better until we were married and saw each other daily," Sister Carmichael said. "We always felt like we were being torn in two when we had to say good-night. I think that's part of the reason we only courted for about two months--we just couldn't stand to be apart. A lot of our parents' friends gave us the 'marry in haste' lecture, but we didn't care, we knew we were doing what was right for us. Just remember how you feel now, if you're ever tempted to part for good. If you can always feel like you're only half a person without the other, it will help you want to do everything in your power to work things out when things get tough."

"Thank you," he told them.

At home everyone just let George have his space, realizing that there wasn't anything they could do to help him. Kurt and Cherish tried to give him extra things to do to keep him busy, Jane asked him to play games with her and go riding, and no one mentioned Alex except to ask how she was doing after she called each evening. He would tell them a little about what she'd done that day, but mostly just that she was fine.

By the time New Year's Day came around, George was more than ready to head back to his apartment, more so than he had been at any other time.

"Thank you Mom, Dad, for a great Christmas. It's always great to come home. I'm sure you'll understand, though, that I'm glad it's time to leave," he told them the night before he flew back to L.A.

"Yes, we understand, dear," Cherish said. "Make sure you let us know how things go with you and Alex, especially if she gets baptized. We'd like to come out if she does."

"I will, Mom. Thank you for showing me the kind of marriage that I want to have. I've seen you work through the hard times, both financial and personal. I'm hoping that Alex's time with us has helped her to see at least a little of what we grew up with, since she lost her parents when she was young."

The time finally came for him to leave for the airport. Jane went with him so that she could drive the jeep back to the house. George kept the conversation going, talking about anything that came to mind, just so he wouldn't think about Alex so much. But she was always there, just below the surface of his conscious thought. At the airport George and Jane gave each other a hug.

"Take care, Squirt. Do your school work and keep the boys at bay," he teased.

"Nah, homework's overrated and the boys, well, if I keep them at bay, how will I find one to marry?"

George gave her a look of mock horror.

"An old maid like you? Who'd marry you?" he joked.

Jane playfully punched him in the arm and George pretended that it hurt.

"With an arm like that, I really will be surprised if you get married," he said with a smile.

Jane dropped her playful demeanor and said seriously, "I hope you and Alex get married. I really feel that she needs us in her life. Don't wait any longer than you need to to propose."

"I don't intend to wait any longer than necessary. I'm trying to do this on the Lord's time. He knows when she'll be ready for that step, and I keep getting the answer that the time hasn't come yet. I'll let everyone know immediately if and when she says yes. Now, I have to get going. I'll talk with you later. Give Starlight, Charlie, and Cinder a lump of sugar for me. I'll call when I get in. Drive safe," he told her.

"Love you, George."

"Love you, too, Squirt."

George's flight was on time but crowded with holiday travelers returning home. Several small children kept parents busy dealing with their crying or attempts to run around the cabin. George sat next to a young mother with a five- or six-year-old who didn't seem to think that sitting by the window and looking out was very exciting, and who kept asking if they were there yet.

George chuckled to himself, thinking that children did not change much. When he was a child, traveling always took longer than he wanted it to as well. He decided to take pity on the young mother.

"Do you mind if I tell him a story?" he asked.

"If you can do anything to keep him quiet and sitting down, please, feel free. He's been like this for the last five hours, and I'm just about worn out with it," she told him.

"Hi, my name is George. Do you like cats?" he asked the boy.

The boy looked at him as if trying to decide if the question was worth answering, but finally nodded solemnly.

"I know a story about four kittens. The black one was named Snowball, the white one was named Midnight, the orange one was named Cinder, and the grey one was named George, like me."

George proceeded to tell the story. The four kittens had asked to go on a picnic, and their mother had said it was okay, but they had to be careful if they went by the big stream as the water moved quickly. The kittens said they would be careful, and then set out with a picnic blanket, a basket of food, a jump rope, and their fishing poles. After arriving at their picnic spot and spreading out their blanket, and took turns jumping rope for a while. When they were tired of that, they decided to go fishing. Each of the kittens caught one or two fish except Snowball, so Snowball decided to climb the tree that was growing next to the water. A branch hung over the water, and by climbing onto it and going to the very end, Snowball could see the fish below. He was so excited when he finally caught a fish, he wasn't paying attention and overbalanced, falling into the water. His brothers and sister knew they had to do something to help, so they grabbed the jump rope and swung it out into the water. Poor Snowball missed the rope. The other three ran up ahead and swung the rope out again. This time Snowball just barely caught the rope with one of his claws. Between climbing the rope and the others pulling him in, he finally reached the shore safely. The other three kittens helped Snowball restore his fur to normal. They decided that since Snowball was safe, they should continue with their picnic, but stay away from the water. When the kittens got home, their mom asked how the picnic had gone. Knowing that it was better to tell the truth than for their mom to find out the truth later, they told her what happened. Even though she was disappointed that Snowball had not listened to her, the mother cat was happy that her kittens were safe, and she snuggled with all of them.

Once the story was over George asked, "Do you know what we can learn from this story?"

The little boy shook his head solemnly.

"We can learn that when our parents tell us we should or shouldn't do something, even if we don't know why, they have a reason for it. Another thing we can learn is that if we get into trouble, we have our family to help us out. But we should do our best to not get into trouble to start with."

The boy looked at his mom and said, "Mommy, can he tell me bedtime stories like that again? I like that story better than the ones you read me."

"Well, dear, I don't think so. George probably has his own home to go to. But tell you what. When we get home, you can help me write a story that you do like, and I will read that to you. Would that be okay?"

The boy tipped his head in contemplation of this offer, and after a minute he nodded and said that would be okay. After this the boy was content to color in his coloring book while he chatted away about the story he wanted to help write when he got home.

"I can't tell you how grateful I am for your help," the child's mother said. "How did you come up with that story? I'm terrible at creative thinking like that. You give me a pad of paper and paints and I have no problem, but to come up with a story on the spur of the moment, well, forget it."

"It's actually a story my mom read to us when we were kids. She had all sorts of stories with morals and we all learned the ones we liked the best. It's called 'The Kittens' Picnic', if you want to try to find it. It's in a collection of books by two or three different authors."

"Thank you, I will look it up. I just hope they're still in print," she said.

The rest of the trip, as far as his traveling companions were concerned, went smoothly. The boy even decided that looking out the window at the small roads, homes, and cars was fun, and he spent several minutes quietly looking at what they were flying over.

Once the plane landed, George waited his turn to disembark and then went to the baggage claim. After he had his luggage, he retrieved his car from the long-term parking lot and drove home. Once home, he unpacked a few essentials, showered, then flopped onto his bed, emotionally and physically exhausted. He was almost asleep when he remembered he still needed to call home and let them know he had arrived okay.

Groggily George checked the time and found that it was only eight p.m. local time. He called his parents, reported that he was home, and told them that he would call them again in a day or two. Next he quickly called Alex and let her know he was home. They talked for a few minutes before Alex said that she would let him go so he could get some sleep. After hanging up, George dragged himself off the bed to say his prayers. He quickly but sincerely thanked the Lord for a safe flight and asked that he would get the rest that he needed. He then crawled back into bed.

The next morning George woke up to sunlight shining in his eyes from the place in the blinds where the slats didn't line up properly. He groaned and rolled over, covering his head with his pillow. He lay there for a few minutes before deciding to at least check the time. He peered through creaking eyelids at his alarm clock. Nine o'clock. Later than he thought it might be, but still earlier than he wanted to be awake. He debated sleepily if he had the energy to get up, and decided he didn't. As he didn't have to be into work until the next day, he decided if he need more sleep he should get it.

The next time George woke up it was after noon. He felt much better, but was still a bit wooly-headed from the stress of not having Alex around. He took a cool shower to try to finish getting rid of his muzzy-headedness, brushed his teeth, and got dressed. He knew there wouldn't be anything in the fridge to eat since he had been gone a month. He picked up his car keys and wallet and went to get groceries and something to eat, not necessarily in that order. For something to eat, he went to his favorite cafe as it served breakfast all day. Once there he ordered two large glasses of orange juice, a stack of sourdough pancakes, a side of corned beef hash, and two sausages. When the orange juice arrived, George drank the first one thirstily, glad for the fresh-squeezed taste that helped wake up his taste buds. He set the almost-empty glass down, then waited patiently for the rest of his food to arrive.

While he waited, he called the office on his cell phone to let Pat know he was home and that he would be coming in the next day as planned. Pat asked how things had gone over Christmas, and George purposely did not make much mention of Alex, telling him instead of his pending change of status to uncle. Pat, of course, was excited for Doug and Nancy, whom he had met several times when they were in college, and for the family as a whole.

Just as Pat asked more pointedly about Alex's being with them for the holidays, George was saved from responding by the arrival of his food.

"I'm sorry, Pat, but my breakfast just showed up and I'm really hungry. I'll catch up with you later," George said.

After hanging up and putting his phone away, George tucked into his food, spreading a liberal amount of butter on each of his pancakes, then drowning them in the homemade boysenberry syrup that the cafe was known for. He was about halfway through the stack of pancakes when Greta, the owner and head cook, came over to see how he was.

"Greta, you've outdone yourself. If I didn't think my mom would somehow find out, I would tell you these are even better than hers. But I know she would, so you'll have to settle for being second best," he said, as he sat back and patted his flat stomach.

"Being second best to your mother is just fine with me if you put it that way," Greta said, smiling.

Greta was a big woman with a ruddy complexion. Her blue eyes twinkled as she talked and her hands fluttered about as if wanting to make something. She always took the time to come out and see how her favorite customers were doing, no matter how busy it was. And anyone who had been there more than three times was likely to be considered a favored customer.

"So how was your Christmas? I haven't seen you in here for about a month, so I'm guessing that you went home this year. How is your family?" she asked.

"Mom and Dad are well enough. Dad had a small heart attack just before I went up and didn't want to tell me beforehand so as not to worry me. But he's decided to slow down and let the foreman and his son do more of the day-to-day running of the ranch and farm. Doug and Nancy found out they're expecting right before Christmas, and so that made a nice surprise for all of us. Jane is just about ready to get married to hear her talk, although I don't think she's dating anyone seriously right now. And I do believe I've found the woman whom I plan on marrying," he said with a sly grin.

"Oh you have not! Your funning me, aren't you? You go away for a month and come back almost engaged? No you didn't," Greta said in disbelief.

"I most certainly did. What's more, it was in the space of less than two weeks. One of our clients wanted me to personally work on her brochure, and she sent her assistant, Alex, over to make sure it was done right. As a reward for all her hard work, Alex got to stay with us until the day after Christmas. It's going to be a long-distance relationship, but if it's to be, it will be," he said happily.

"Well, congratulations. Let me know if the lady says yes, and you'll get breakfast on the house," Greta told him warmly.

"I will," he said.

"I need to get back to the kitchen so I'll talk with you later, yes?"

"Yes, I'll see you later. Have a good day."

Once Greta was back in the kitchen, George heard her tell Hector, her soft-spoken husband and second in command, "That George, he's going to get married soon. No, not engaged yet, but soon!"

George shook his head in amusement at Greta's reaction, finished eating, and then paid his bill. From the restaurant he went to the grocery store and bought enough food for the next two weeks.

After returning home and putting the groceries away, George took out his patriarchal blessing. He read over it, paying particular attention to certain parts. He had always been glad to have these direct instructions from the Lord, as they served to remind him that if he kept doing what was right, regardless of how hard it seemed at the time, the promised blessings would be fulfilled. Today he was looking for guidance on his choice of wife. He read the pertinent parts of the blessing and tried to understand their deeper meaning. He read those parts two or three times, letting the guidance sink in, before putting the blessing away and taking out his scriptures.

George read for half an hour, then feeling restless, decided to go for a walk around a nearby park. He grabbed a light jacket and headed out. The park was not big, but big enough that after walking around it twice he was ready to sit down. Before going home he sat on a bench and watched a couple of teenage boys play one-on-one basketball for a while. Once home, George put in a movie and lay down on the couch to watch it.

About halfway through the movie, he got the phone call he had been waiting for since he first woke up.

"Hello, Sweetheart," he said as he answered the phone.

"Hi. How are you today? Get enough sleep?" Alex asked.

"Yes, I think I did. I ended up sleeping until after noon, but I felt much the better for it. How was your day?"

"It went well. I was able to catch a big mistake before it became a problem or before Mrs. Hagerman found out about it from another source."

"I'm glad to hear that. So, now that I'm back, I was thinking that we should start planning on which of us will travel to the other first. I'm willing to come up next weekend; it'll take about a week for me to feel like I can leave. If you can recommend a motel close to you, I'll make a reservation in the next day or two," he said.

"Why don't you just stay with me and save the money on a motel?"

"I appreciate the offer, but I feel it's better that we don't stay at each other's places until we're married. It might seem old-fashioned, but at my parents' we had chaperones, but now we won't. When you come here, you can either stay at a motel, or I can arrange for you to stay with a family from church. I know it might feel kind of weird staying with a family you don't know, but I can think of one or two families who would love to have you stay with them while you're here visiting me. I'm sorry that I didn't think to talk about this with you before," George told her, hoping that Alex would understand and appreciate what he was saying.

The line was silent for a minute, and George wasn't sure if the connection had been lost or if Alex was just taking in what he had said. He was just about to ask if she was still there when she responded.

"Thank you, George. I appreciate what you've told me. I don't know any other guy who wouldn't just assume that he would stay at my place, or who would care what it looked like. If the people from your church are anything like your parents, I would be happy to stay with them. Have I told you today that I love you?"

"Not yet, but now's a good time," he said, smiling in relief at her response. "I love you, too."

They talked for another half hour.

"I have to get to bed so I can get up for work tomorrow," George said. "I'll call you tomorrow night. About what time should I call?"

"If you call around nine, that should be good. I have some errands to run after work and I don't expect to be home until about then."

"Nine, then. Sleep well, my love"

"You, too. Good-night."

"'Night," he said and reluctantly disconnected the call.

Chapter 10

George spent the next week catching up at work. They had contracts with two new clients, and this required a great deal of research on the clients' previous ad work to see what had already been tried. Pat tried to extract more information from George about Alex and him, but George put him off with vague answers and continued to work tirelessly on the new campaigns.

Once he got home, George took care of his mail and personal phone calls, and then cook dinner if he had enough energy, or order take-out if he didn't. Then he would take a deep breath and call Alex. He and Alex talked for about half an hour every night.

One night Alex told George that she was about halfway through First Nephi and was praying like Sister Tan had asked her to do. George related some of his missionary experiences, and Alex listened eagerly.

When Friday night finally came, George had a weekend bag and camera gear packed and in his car so he could leave directly from work. He said a quick prayer before he left asking for safe travel. He stopped at a fast-food place for dinner, then headed north on I-5 until it connected with CA-99. When he was about halfway to Placerville he called Alex to let her know where he was. He arrived at his hotel about one a.m., and he barely got into bed after saying his prayers before falling asleep.

The next morning George heard a knock at his door. When he got up to answer it, he glanced at the clock and saw that it was eight o'clock. Since he wasn't expecting anyone, he asked who it was.

"Room service," the person answered.

Confused, he opened the door, intending to tell the person they had the wrong room.

"I'm sorry, but I didn't order—Alex! Come here, woman," he said, pulling her close and giving her a kiss.

Once George was satisfied that it was really Alex and not a figment of his imagination, he ushered her inside the room.

"I wasn't expecting you to show up. I'm afraid since I got in so late that I overslept. I need to take a shower and get dressed. If you'll give me about fifteen minutes, I'll be ready to go," he told her.

"I'll wait," she said.

He gathered his clothes and toiletries and then went into the bathroom. He sang with joy as he showered. Once he was done with his shower, he quickly dried off and dressed. Once he was dressed, he opened the door to let the steam escape before brushing his teeth. In too much of a hurry to be with Alex, he skipped shaving. He got his wallet and car keys, keycard, and camera case, and they left.

"Your car or mine?" he asked.

"Mine. It's my turn to show you around."

They got in Alex's car. She drove to a twenty-four hour diner, and they went in to have breakfast.

"Have you been here before?" George asked.

"Every Saturday. They have a killer special," she said as they walked inside.

Once seated they both ordered fresh squeezed orange juice and two breakfast specials without even looking at the menu. Then they just smiled at each other and held hands on the table top, happy to be together again after three weeks apart. Breakfast came but George was barely aware that he ate at all, he was so happy at

125

being with Alex again. He pushed away the thought that they would be together for less than forty-eight hours.

After a mostly silent breakfast George asked, "So, what do you have planned for today?"

"I have a couple of surprises for you. First, we're going to go over to the resort. Mrs. Hagerman threatened to fire me if I didn't bring you by to say hi."

"I'd love that. It's been too long since I saw her."

They drove the hour to the resort, listening to music and talking. Once they arrived at the resort, Alex parked in the employee lot, and they got out. George took his camera case with him and followed Alex inside the main building. He had been to the resort once or twice before while working on jobs for Mrs. Hagerman, but he never tired of seeing the buildings. Hagerman's Retreat was well known for its rustic charm, magnificent views, and access to some of the area's best winter and summer activities.

Alex led him to Mrs. Hagerman's office.

"I called ahead to give her an idea of what time we'd be here, and she said to check the office first," Alex said, knocking on the door.

"Come in," Mrs. Hagerman said.

George opened the door and let Alex precede him into the office.

"George, good you see you, boy. How are you doing?" Mrs. Hagerman said, getting up from her desk and coming over to shake his hand.

"I'm well, ma'am, thank you. And how are you doing? I'm glad you like the layout we did," George said.

"Love it. One of the best brochures I think you boys have done so far. I just might use the template for a while and just change the information as needed. I'm well, thank you.

"I've been told that you and Alex hit it off quite well. I'm glad. I've been waiting to hear that you and Pat have started to settle down, but that news has never come. When I called Pat and he told me you were on vacation, I thought that sending Alex to help get the layout done properly was a great idea. And yes, Alex, I did have this in mind when I sent you--no need to get your feathers ruffled."

126

George started to chuckle and then broke into full laughter. Alex looked at him with a somewhat miffed expression on her face. They made eye contact, and she started to laugh as well.

When George had calmed down, he pulled Alex to his side and gave her a squeeze.

"Mrs. H., I would never have suspected that you were behind this. I knew Pat was up to something when I found out that Alex wasn't a guy like he had purposely led me to believe, but never once did I think that you were in on this. Well, you got me good on this one, and I have to say I'm happy about your butting into my love life," George told the older woman as he looked at Alex and smiled.

"I still think that it wasn't her place to play matchmaker," Alex grumbled to George, "even if it did turn out okay."

"Don't worry about it, dear. I did the same thing with your predecessor, and her predecessor. But don't you dare tell anyone or I'll deny it," Mrs. Hagerman said, straightening to her somehow impressive full four foot ten inches.

"We wouldn't dream of telling anyone, Mrs. H. But you do realize that we haven't gotten to the point of really talking marriage yet, don't you? Right now we're still trying to get to know one another," George said.

"Well, of course I know that! Do you think I've gone batty and don't know everything thing that I want to know? Well, okay, there are things I don't know, but not about the people I want to see together," Mrs. Hagerman said smugly.

George threw up his hands in surrender. "Okay Mrs. H., have it your way."

"Well, children, I need to get back to work. Feel free to hang around for a bit. Alex tells me that you play the piano. If you want to, you can play the one in the main lounge. You know that the guests love to have someone playing," Mrs. Hagerman said, extending her hand to shake George's.

"Thank you for having me over for a visit. The piano is a great idea, thank you."

Alex and George took their leave and headed to the main lounge. George checked the piano bench, but there wasn't any music in it.

127

"I know some songs by heart, but other than at my parents' place I haven't played much. Do you know where there might be some sheet music?" he asked Alex.

"Sure. Give me a minute or two and I'll be right back."

While she was gone, George ran through some warm-up exercises and was playing a hymn when Alex returned.

"Here you go," she said, putting the music on the piano's holder.

"Thanks," he said, finishing up the song.

There were about a half dozen people in the lounge, all doing their own thing, but George could tell that they were listening to the music. He looked through the music that Alex had found and chose a couple of songs he felt comfortable with. Alex sat on the piano bench next to him and turned pages for him. He played for about an hour before getting tired. A couple of the people who had been in the lounge came and complimented him how well he played. George thanked them and smiled when they asked if he would be back later to play some more.

"No, I'm a business associate of the owner, just up for the weekend. The owner said that if I wanted to play, I could. I might be back next month, but I'm not sure."

"We'll look forward to your coming back," one of them told him.

Once he had finished playing they drove from the resort to Placerville where they got gas.

"Okay, you have a couple of choices. I wasn't sure what you would want to do, so I looked up a couple things on the Internet. There's an aquarium and aviary, a small film festival, or a natural history museum we can go to," Alex offered.

"Oh, that's a tough choice. Hmm," George said and thought for a few seconds. "I think the aquarium and aviary. I'm not much for film festivals since I never know in advance if the movies will be ones I'd want to see, and sometimes I find out too late that I don't want to be watching a particular one. The museum we can do next time."

"Okay then, animals it is."

They drove and talked about anything or nothing as they felt compelled to share pieces of their past. They also discussed plans for Alex's visit to L.A. in a couple of weeks. Once at the aquarium and aviary, they approached the ticket booth.

"Welcome to Animals of Air and Water. We have a special today—if you buy a ticket for each, the second set of tickets are half-price," the ticket seller told them.

"We'll have two tickets for both, then. Thank you," Alex said.

They went to the aviary first, and George took pictures of the birds that caught his interest. In one of the shots, he had Alex stand so that it looked like the bird behind her was sitting on her hand. They laughed at how funny looking some of the birds were. They took turns making up funny stories about why they looked the way they did.

Alex finally could stand it no longer.

"Stop! We...have to...stop! Are you... trying to...make me wet my pants? I don't...have any back ups...with me," she told him as she gasped for breath.

George grinned at her, but stopped the story he was in the process of telling.

They finished their aviary visit and went inside to the aquarium. This time George refrained from telling stories, but it was one of the hardest things he had ever done, aside from not proposing to Alex. They held hands, took pictures from time to time, and just enjoyed being together.

After leaving the aquarium they went to lunch at a New York-style pizza place. They ordered large slices of thin-crust pizza with their favorite toppings. Alex had tomato and spinach on hers, while George had everything, including anchovies, on his.

"How can you eat those things?" Alex asked, referring to the anchovies.

"Easy, one bite at a time," he said, smirking.

Alex playfully hit him on the arm.

"Seriously, they're awful," she said.

"Well, growing up I thought that too. But when I was on my mission, my companion dared me to eat a medium-size pizza with nothing but anchovies on it. Being the macho twenty-year-old that I was, I did it. By the time I was half-way through that pizza, I loved anchovies, and my companion never dared me to eat anything again."

"You're making that up," Alex said in disbelief.

"It's the truth. If you don't believe me, I can give you his number. Max would love to talk with you again, I'm sure," George told her.

"Max--from Sun Valley? I thought you went to college together."

"We did. We went to our first year of college together, then ended up in the same mission and were companions for about six months. The fact that we were already friends made being missionary companions easier. Then after our missions, we were back at college again. We were always bumping into one another."

They finished lunch and then drove back to Alex's place, stopping on the way to grab groceries for George to cook for dinner. Once at Alex's apartment they popped in an old black and white Cary Grant movie and cuddled on the couch. After the movie George made a simple dinner of spaghetti with corn on the cob and a salad. Alex chopped the vegetables for the salad and set the table. After dinner they played a couple hands of cards before George decided it was time to go.

"I'll pick you up for church if you want. I already have the information for the ward you would be in," he offered.

"That would be great. I haven't taken the time to go yet. Is it going to be like your church at home?"

"That's one of the best things about our church—it is the same everywhere in the world there's a branch or ward. We all use the same lesson manuals, sing the same songs, though maybe in different languages, and use the same sets of scriptures. Sometimes one ward might be a lesson ahead or behind another ward, but that's about it."

"What time will you be here, then?"

"About eight-thirty. That way we'll have plenty of time to get there and maybe even have a chance to talk with the missionaries in your ward or with the bishop."

They hugged and George gave her a quick kiss.

"I'll see you in the morning, then," he said as he opened the door. "Sleep well. I love you."

"I love you. Drive safely."

130

The next morning George checked out of the hotel and was knocking on Alex's door at eight-thirty on the dot. Alex opened the door then finished putting in an earring. She was dressed in the blue silk suit he had first seen her in, and she had the top section of her hair pulled back in a clip.

"Good morning, beautiful," he said to her, giving her a quick kiss.

"Good morning yourself, handsome," she responded, smiling.

"Are you ready to go? I checked how long it should take to get to the meeting house, and we have a minute or two if you're not quite ready."

"Let me just put some lipstick on and I'll be ready."

George waited in the front room while Alex put the finishing touches on her makeup. She grabbed her purse and Book of Mormon, and then they left.

The church parking lot was fairly empty as it was still about ten minutes before the first meeting started, so they found a good spot near one of the side doors. George retrieved his scriptures from the back seat and the two of them were about half way to the door when he slapped his forehead with the heel of his hand.

"I forgot something," he said as he turned around.

Alex followed and stood next to George as he opened the trunk. He pulled out two wrapped packages, one the size of a small box and the other a bit larger, but squishy.

"George, you need to stop getting things for me! I'm going to get spoiled," Alex complained, half-heartedly.

"I can't see you getting spoiled, Sweetheart. But if you do, that's okay, too, if it's on my love," he said, smiling at her.

She opened the odd package first and found a scripture carrier. The other package contained a Bible, and a Doctrine and Covenants/Pearl of Great Price.

"Now you'll have your own set of scriptures to use in church and to read at home. I didn't know whether you had a Bible, and even if you did, I thought you might want the one the church uses that is cross-referenced to all the other scriptures."

Alex carefully put all the scriptures in the carrier, set it on the trunk of the car, and gave George a big hug.

131

"You are too good for me," she said from inside his arms, his cheek resting on the top of her head.

"I don't believe anything is too good for you," he said, pulling back to look at her seriously. "Now let's get inside and find out where we should go."

Alex grabbed her new scripture case with one hand and took George's hand with the other as they walked inside.

At the chapel doors an older woman greeted them and gave them a program for Sacrament Meeting.

"Welcome to the ward. Is this your first time here?" the greeter asked them.

"Yes. I'm visiting my girlfriend, Alex, and she's investigating the church. My name is George. We were hoping to see the missionaries or possibly the bishop before the meeting started."

"I'm Sister Hall. Glad you could come to church today. I just saw the missionaries go that way," she said, pointing up the hall.

George and Alex went in the direction that had been indicated, and as they rounded a corner they almost bumped right into the missionaries.

"Sorry, Elders," George said to the young men. "We were trying to find you, not run you down."

George explained the situation to the elders.

The Elders introduced themselves then set up an appointment with Alex for later that week before offering to introduce her to the Relief Society president and bishop. Alex accepted their offer and she and George followed the missionaries into the chapel. There they were quickly introduced to the bishop. As it was almost time for Sacrament Meeting to start, they found places and sat down.

During Sacrament Meeting George felt a sense of rightness and peace. This feeling helped lift him from the funk caused by his having to have a long-distance relationship with Alex. He knew that if the Lord had put Alex in his life, it was for His purposes. He would just have to have patience and faith, and hope that things would turn out the way he wanted them to, but be accepting if they didn't.

After Sacrament Meeting, the Elders introduced Alex and George to the Relief Society president, Sister Havensworth. Sister Havensworth readily agreed to help Alex in any way she could. Alex and George then went to their Sunday school class, and afterwards split for their respective Priesthood and Relief Society meetings.

Once church was over Alex and George were introduced to a few more people. Alex commented to the group they had just met, "George told me that your church was the same everywhere in the world, but I didn't really believe him. I've been to other churches, and while the same sorts of things were taught, I never felt that they actually believed the same thing. I feel like in your church it really is the same, although I've only been to two sets of meetings."

"I know what you mean," A Sister Jacobs said. "I joined the church after looking into it for six months. It took that long partly because I was having problems with housing and jobs, and I moved around to four different wards in two different states. Because the Church was the same in each of those places, it was easier for me to focus on what I was learning and feeling the Spirit as I moved around. I've never regretted my decision to join the Church, not even when my family threatened to disown me. I decided if it's God's church, I needed to do what He wants me to do, and not be held back by my family."

"Did they disown you?" Alex asked, concerned.

"Yes, they did. Until I gave them grandchildren, that is," she said, smiling.

The women gave Alex their phone numbers just in case Alex needed anything. Alex thanked them and she and George returned to the car.

"They are so nice, George. I'm really glad you belong to this church. Even though we won't be able to see each other much right now, I think all I'll have to do is come to church or talk to one of the members, and I'll feel like you're here with me," Alex said.

"I'm glad to hear that," George replied. "One of my concerns has been that with my not being around, you might find it harder to continue learning about the church. If you ever need help with anything, give any of them a call. If they can't help you themselves, they will direct you to someone who can."

"I'll keep that in mind. Thank you."

Back at Alex's place George changed out of his dress shirt before his long drive home. He asked if there was anything he could do to help with lunch since he needed to leave as soon as possible in order to get home at a decent time.

"I'm not sure. I'm trying to start my cooking at a beginner's level with macaroni and cheese. I think I can manage that without help," she said with a smile.

George sat down at the table and looked around Alex's apartment. He spotted the figurines he and his father had given her for Christmas on top of the microwave. He went over and picked up the music box and wound it. The classical music filled the room. George pulled Alex into a waltz that was slightly hampered by the small space. Alex gave a little shriek of surprise when he grabbed her, but happily fell into step, and they danced until the music stopped.

"Sorry," he said with a crooked smile. "I just couldn't help myself."

"I'm glad. I enjoyed the dancing. I haven't done any in a long time," Alex said, smiling as she went back to preparing lunch.

After lunch George said his good-byes and started on the six-hour drive back to L.A. On the way home he listened to his favorite CDs, feeling much better about where he and Alex were going with their relationship and her learning more about the church.

Chapter 11

At the office the next day, Pat finally cornered George.

"Okay, what gives? Last week you looked like you had lost your best friend, and this week you're whistling around the office. This has to do with Alex—I won't believe anything else," Pat told him, perching on the corner of his desk.

George grinned at Pat as he leaned back in his chair with his fingers laced behind his head.

"What do you want to know?" George asked.

Pat stared at him in surprise for a couple seconds.

"You gave in way too easily, George old buddy, after evading me all last week but I'll take it. I want to know if you and Alex hit it off, and why the difference between last week and today."

George considered the question for a bit before responding.

"Did Alex and I hit it off? You could say so. The difference between last week and today? I went to visit her over the weekend. That's all."

"That's all? That's--. No, you don't get away with that. I can tell it's more than that. If you hit it off, that makes it sound like you two are just friends who get along with each other. If you're visiting her on the weekend already, that's more like you're dating. You are, aren't you?" George grinned even wider, and Pat got up and came around the desk to slug him in the shoulder. "You sly dog! And here I thought you just wanted to go back and visit with your folks some more, or that you had a bad case of indigestion."

"Yes, we're dating. We've talked every night since she left. I would have gone up last weekend too, but I had just gotten back and felt like I needed to get caught up before leaving again, even for just the weekend," George told him.

"We'll have to go out to celebrate. This is your first girlfriend since high school, if I'm not mistaken."

"Well, second girlfriend. You forgot about Barbra Jean."

"Oh, heavens. I would like to forget about Barbra Jean. She was just short of psycho! You almost didn't graduate because she took the one term paper that you needed the most and she wouldn't give it back to you."

"I'm sure glad you talked her into giving it back to me in time for me to finish it. I still don't know how you managed to do that. I talked to her until I was blue in the face, and all she would say was that if I graduated, I would leave and then we wouldn't be able to be together."

"I told her that if she didn't give you the paper back that there was no way that you would stay with her, but if she gave it back, she still had a smidgen of a chance with you. It was the only thing I could think of that might get her to realize that what she was doing was counterproductive. Fortunately for you it worked, even if you did have to get a restraining order on her.

"So, you're dating Alex now. How far have things gone? Should I get my tux dry cleaned and start rehearsing my best man speech?"

George shook his head slowly and said, "No, not yet. Alex is looking into the church right now, and I feel that she needs to work out some issues before I propose. But the topic of marriage has been brought up and Alex hasn't run away screaming, so I have hope. The first time she told me that she loved me was right in front of everyone, after she opened the Christmas gifts I had bought her."

"Wow, what did you get her? I'll have to remember for the next time I want a girl to tell me she loves me."

"I don't think it'd work for you, buddy-boy. I gave her a couple of glass figurines she had been admiring at Sun Valley."

"Nope, not likely to work, but you never know. Well, now that I have satisfied my curiosity somewhat, I'll let you get back to work. I'll grill you more over dinner tonight."

With these parting remarks, Pat left, and George returned to working on the layout in front of him.

At dinner that night George told Pat almost everything that had happened. He omitted only those things Alex had told him about her past.

"Wow, that's incredible. Do you have a picture of her with you?" Pat asked.

George gave him a look of condescension.

"Of course I have a picture of her with me. I'm the photographer, aren't I?"

"Silly me. Of course."

George pulled his wallet out of his pocket and took out the requested picture.

Pat's eyes almost bulged out of his head and he looked up incredulously.

"You mean I had the opportunity to meet her before you did, and I passed it up? Would that be incredible stupidity on my part, or just dumb luck on yours?" Pat asked, shaking his head as he handed the picture back.

"I'll call it the Lord's hand in things," George said, smiling as he looked at the picture briefly before putting it away.

"You've got that right. No one but the Lord would have put you two together. From this picture it looks like she's way outta your league."

"Yes, but that's okay. She still loves me," George said with a sigh.

"You've got it bad, don't you?" Pat asked.

George just smiled.

The next weekend that they could get together, Alex drove down to L.A. George had made arrangements for her to stay at the Relief Society president's house. Sister Snow and her husband were an older couple whose children were grown and no longer living at home. Being a romantic, Sister Snow was very happy to help further someone else's love life. Besides, George was something of a favorite of hers due to his willingness to help out whenever asked.

"You have a girlfriend? That's wonderful. We'd be delighted to have her stay with us for the weekend. Will she be coming to church, or will she have to drive back before then?"

"Since our ward has the nine o'clock block, Alex will be able to come to church with me before she heads back."

"I'm glad to hear it," Sister Snow said.

Even though it was really late when Alex finally arrived at George's, she followed him to the Snows' house. She and Sister Snow hit it off immediately, so George felt even better about the arrangement and left Alex to get some sleep.

At about eight the next morning, George showed up at the Snows' with a bouquet of flowers in a cut glass vase. Sister Snow opened the door at his knock.

"George! Glad to see you. Come in. Oh, those are beautiful. She's going to love them," she said. "I'll let her know—oh, here she is."

Alex came around the corner and stopped short when she saw the flowers. George could see the tears well up in her eyes.

"Aww, Sweetheart, don't cry," he said as he hurried over to her. "I know that you'll have to take them back with you, but I thought they would be nice in your room now. They'll remind you of me."

Sister Snow thoughtfully took the arrangement from George so he could hug Alex.

"You're pretty much all I do think about," Alex said. "Mrs. Hagerman has even commented on it. Not that I got in trouble or anything, but I need to make sure that when I'm at work my mind is on the job," she said as he held her against his chest.

"Do you want to ease up on seeing each other, so you can have some space?" George asked, although not sure if he would be

138

able to handle their seeing even less of one another than they did now.

"No, just the opposite. All I can think about is how long it's going to be until we see each other again. Or the things I'm learning from church or the missionaries. I'm understanding things in a whole new light."

George chuckled, "Well, right now there's not much I can do to help with that. I don't think right now is the best time to make any major decisions, like moving. Maybe in a couple of months, when we have a better idea if this relationship is going to be as long-term as I would like it to be."

Sister Snow cleared her throat, and George and Alex turned toward her, embarrassed that they had once again forgotten they were not alone.

"I'll just put these in your room, Alex, and let you two love birds be on your way. Let me get you a key first," Sister Snow said before going into the other room.

"She's great," Alex said. "We stayed up talking for about half an hour last night. She told me a little about how she met her husband and the problems they had. She was engaged to someone else when she met and fell in love with Brother Snow, and they had to find a legitimate way for her to break off the engagement."

"I know. Every Valentine's Day they have a group of single people from church over for dinner and they give an abridged version of it. Three years running I've been invited since I'm one of the most eligible bachelors in the ward."

"I believe that," Alex said, standing on tiptoe to give him a kiss.

"Here you go, here's the key. It took me a minute to find it," Sister Snow said as she came around the corner.

Alex took the key, put it on her key ring so she wouldn't lose it, then left with George.

"Any ideas where you want to go?" he asked once they were in the car.

"I don't know. This is your stomping ground," she said.

"How about Knott's Berry Farm or Disneyland? And there's the wax museum, or just about anything you can think of."

Alex thought for a bit and then said, "I went to a wax museum once a long time ago, but Knott's or Universal Studios would be nice. If I'm going to go to Disneyland, I want to have a couple of days. Maybe I can take Friday off the next time I come down, and we can do Disneyland on Friday and Saturday, if that works for you."

"Sounds like a plan. We might not be able to do it for a couple of months, though. Universal Studios is closer, so let's go there today," he said, starting the car.

Due to the traffic, it took them about an hour to get to Universal Studios. They parked in a parking garage close to the park and went to buy their tickets.

After they had their tickets, Alex asked George if he had brought his camera.

"No. I didn't want to be carrying it around an amusement park all day and maybe damaging it," he said.

Once inside the park, they decided to proceed counterclockwise and do all the rides. They laughed with nostalgia as they went on rides for E.T. and some of the movie scenes like where the shark from Jaws pops up at the tourists. They looked at the movie star memorabilia, ate lunch, and then went back for more. When they had finished all the rides, they ate dinner at Pinks, which was famous for its hotdogs named after movies and movie stars.

Completely exhausted, but happy, they headed back to L.A., Alex cuddling the stuffed bear that George had won for her. By the time they got to the Snows', Alex had fallen asleep. George parked the car and watched her for a minute. His heart beat with a love for her that he had no way of expressing adequately. He got out of the car and went around to her side.

"Wake up, Sleeping Beauty. I'd try to carry you, but I'd have to get you out and find the key," he said as he gently shook her.

Alex stirred groggily but stayed asleep. He leaned across her and unbuckled her seatbelt, carefully retracting it. He found the key ring in her purse, went to the door and spent a couple of minutes trying to figure out which was the right key. Once he got the door unlocked, George went back to the car and found Alex finally waking up.

"Careful, Love, let me help you," he said, helping her stand up. He took her purse and the teddy bear in one arm and wrapped his other arm firmly around her waist.

"I'm awake," she mumbled.

"Not so much that I trust you not to fall if I let go," he said.

By the time they were inside the house, Alex was awake. At the door he gave her a hug and a brief kiss.

"I love you, sleep well. I'll be over to get you about a quarter to nine. Or you can ride to church with the Snows if you prefer," he said.

"You can get me," she said through a yawn, stretching.

"Okay. See you in the morning, Sweetheart. Lock up after me," he said, handing her the house key.

"I will. 'Night."

George waited to hear the lock click before getting into his car and driving home.

The next morning George arrived a few minutes early. Alex opened the door when he rang the doorbell, and once again she took his breath away. She was wearing her forest green chenille sweater shirt with a knee-length black leather skirt and knee-high black leather boots.

"Woman, you trying to kill me? Every time I see you I can't breathe for how good you look," he told her, standing back to look at her.

Alex blushed and said, "I don't have much in the way of church clothes, and I haven't had much time to go shopping yet."

"Just keep wearing what you have and I'll be happy. Of course, I'll have to beat the other guys off with a stick, but that's a small price to pay to have the best-looking woman in town on my arm."

Alex laughed, which was what George had intended. He stepped inside the house while Alex got her scriptures and purse.

"Any surprises today?" she asked cheekily as they got into the car.

"Would it be much of a surprise if I gave you something every time we saw each other?" he asked.

"Of course it would. I still wouldn't know what it was until I opened it," she said with a grin.

"You, my dear, are incorrigible," he said, shaking his head sorrowfully, starting the car.

"That's your fault. I've never been given so many presents in such a short space of time. With my last boyfriend, I was lucky that he remembered my birthday. And he didn't get me anything, just took me to dinner. Of course, that was the night I broke up with him. There were enough things that weren't going well between us at that point that I decided to give myself a present and get rid of him."

"His loss was definitely my gain. Where can I send him a thank-you card?" George joked.

The thought of Alex with anyone else sent panic coursing through his body. He had not thought of it before, but a beautiful woman like Alex must have had boyfriends before. Not that he was jealous--she was with him now and that was what mattered--it was the thought of his not being with her that scared the bajeebers out of him.

After church, George introduced Alex to a few of his friends in the ward.

"For just starting to learn about the church, you have a really good grasp of what the gospel is about," Sister Hallowbrook told Alex.

"Thank you. I wasn't sure if I should say anything in class, but it was like it was going to burst out of me if I didn't," Alex said.

"Dear, that would be the Spirit talking. People feel it in different ways, and it's important to learn to recognize how *you* feel the Spirit so you can respond to it accordingly. Right now you may only feel it once in a while since you haven't been baptized and given the gift of the Holy Ghost. But if and when you are baptized and given the gift of the Holy Ghost, you'll be able to have the Spirit with you always if you do what's right. I know it's kind of hard to comprehend right now, and even most of us who were raised in the church don't fully understand how amazing and wonderful this gift is. But we all know it's important that we have the Spirit's guidance when we're making decisions or facing challenges that seem impossible to get through," Sister Geoff said.

After a few more minutes George and Alex went back to the Snows' so Alex could thank them for their hospitality and return the key they had loaned her. George waited in the kitchen with Sister Snow while she put together a quick lunch of ham sandwiches for them. Alex had tried to protest, but Sister Snow had brushed her protests away, telling her it was nice to have someone to do things for. So in the end Alex had given up and gone to the bedroom to get her things. Sister Snow had just finished the sandwiches when Alex returned.

"Thank you, Sister Snow for letting me stay with you. I'm not sure when I'll be down next, but if you wouldn't mind, I'd like to stay with you again. I would feel better staying with the same people from trip to trip versus feeling like I'm imposing on several people. Oh dear, that's not quite what I meant, but you understand, don't you?" Alex asked, concern in her voice.

"Yes, dear, I do understand. You start to get to know someone and then get shuffled off to someone else, and even if they're all nice, it can be unsettling. I had to do that when I was a child after my parents died of scarlet fever. My brothers and sisters and I were all split up and sent back and forth between relatives, depending on who could afford to keep us for a while. We finally ended up being adopted by a couple of families in town who were Church members. They felt bad that we kept being moved around and weren't really being cared for properly. We had gone a whole year without being in school for more than a couple weeks at a time. Back then missing school wasn't a terribly big thing, but we all liked school and missed the learning. Anyway, my point is that I do understand, and that you're more than welcome to stay here when you're in town. Now, eat your lunch so you can get going. I don't know how you drive all that way in one go, but then, you're a lot younger than me. Go on you two, eat," she told them and left the room.

Alex blessed the food and they ate. Afterwards they put Alex's few bags and the flowers in her car.

"I wish you didn't have to go," George told her as he held her.

"I wish I didn't have to go either. But as you said, now's not the time to be making big decisions, like moving."

"We could both pray about it, you know. Maybe this is the time and we just don't know it because we haven't thought to ask," he said, pulling back to look her in the eye. "Will you pray about it and see if you get an answer that one of us should move? It seems to make more sense for you to move since Pat and I have our business here, but I'll move if it's the right thing for us."

"Yes, I will."

They held each other for a few more minutes before George pulled away. Without another word Alex got into her car and waved sadly to George. George waved back just as sadly. He heaved a sigh of loss seeing her go, but hoped that they would soon be together again.

The next month raced by so fast George could barely catch his breath. For the first time in the history of their company Pat and George had almost more clients than they could handle. They hired two more people and started talking about moving to a bigger building.

"Thompson and Jared are sharing an office and so are Johnson and Gomez, and there's almost not enough room for two to an office," Pat told George.

"Maybe you and I should share an office. Johnson and Gomez have less space than the other two, so they could move into my office and then Thompson and Jared could each have their own," George suggested. "That would mean that we'll be kinda crowded, but then we wouldn't have rent a new space."

"I don't know. We've talked about getting a better location if we could afford it. Now might be the time to do that. And you know that if we are sharing the same room it will look bad when clients come and see us crowded together."

"You have a point. Do you have time to look for a new place? I'm rather busy with the projects I have going, but I guess I could spare some time if push came to shove."

"We could take turns. You take half a day to look, and I take half a day. We trade off on Saturdays or something."

"That would probably work," George said.

Pat and George asked Janice, the secretary they shared, for contact information for the realtor that helped them find their current location. Pat called her and the next day the three of them had a preliminary meeting to discuss budget and location preferences. Pat took the first look around and visited three different places. George took the next shift and was able to squeeze in four places that were fairly close to one another, about a half

144

hour south of their current location. One of those seemed promising, but after Pat looked at it they decided it would require more renovation to make it usable than they could afford at the moment. So they continued to look. George sacrificed his weekend with Alex and spent most of Saturday tramping around the valley trying to find a workable office. Either he or Pat would find a place that looked right, but when the other looked at it, something was always wrong with it. Both were about to give up when they realized they had forgotten the most important element; they had forgotten to pray about it. The next Sunday they both fasted and prayed that if they were to find a new location that they would be guided to it. On Monday they called their realtor and asked if there were any new listings or any listings that might be slightly outside the parameters they had originally specified. The realtor silently tapped away at her computer for a few moments.

"There is one here that might work for you. It was just listed five minutes ago, so no one's had a chance to look at it yet. It has about five hundred square feet more than your current location, but is slightly higher than your original price range. It's east of your current place and is on the ninth floor of an older ten-story building. If you want, I can meet one of you over there in about twenty-five minutes," she said, giving George the address.

"That will work. And I think we can both come," George said. He covered the mouthpiece and asked Pat. "Pat, do you think you can come with me to look at this one? It's about ten miles east of here."

"Sure. The kiddies can play by themselves for a while. I'll let Janice know we'll be out and to forward any important calls."

"Yes, we can both make it. We'll meet you over there," George told the realtor.

The lights were with them, so about twenty minutes later Pat and George arrived at the other building. Standing out front of the older style building, George and Pat looked at each other and grinned. This building spoke to both of them. They had arrived before the realtor so they had a few minutes to talk.

"You feel it, too?" Pat asked.

"Yes, I do. Look at that architecture. It's wonderful. I love older buildings, even if they are in less attractive neighborhoods.

They seem to have more character. I think this one is just missing a gargoyle or two, but that's about it. From the outside anyway."

The realtor arrived and took them inside. They took the elevator to the ninth floor and the realtor led them to the appropriate office. She began rattling off information about the building and the area, but George and Pat were not really listening. George did catch that the building had been kept up to code and that the businesses in the building seemed to be very successful and long- standing, and that they were lucky there was an available office to look at.

George and Pat stood in the middle of the open floor and turned around, feeling the spirit of the place. After a few minutes they walked over to the two closed offices and each entered one.

Almost simultaneously they exclaimed, "Wow, would you look at that view!"

Quickly George went to check with Pat and found Pat standing in his doorway, coming to see him.

Grinning from ear to ear, George and Pat turned to the realtor who was standing a few feet away.

"Well take it," they said in unison, and then laughed.

"Okay, let's get the paperwork started. This place won't be on the market for long and you'll want to get your bid in first," she said.

"Do you have the paperwork with you?" Pat asked.

"Yes, here it is," she said, handing it to them.

They sat on the floor and asked for pens, which the realtor supplied. They spent the next ten minutes filling out the required forms and handed them back to her.

"I'll get these in right away, and you should hear from me in about twenty-four to forty-eight hours. If you haven't, give my office a call and we'll check on it."

George and Pat drove back to the office.

"Can you believe it? It just opened up, and all the other businesses are long-standing. If they all do well there, that might mean it's a good location. I wonder why?" Pat asked.

"Don't know, don't much care. The Lord directed us to it and that's all that really matters. It means that we will need to keep up the active client list, but I'm thinking that's not going to be a problem. And with the open floor plan, if we need to hire a couple of more people, we can do it without worrying that anyone will be cramped," George said.

Back at the office they broke the good news to everyone.

"You mean no more shuffling around one another to get to the filing cabinets?" Johnson asked.

"No more tripping over our supplies?" Jared asked.

"Nope and nope. There's even enough room that if we need to hire a couple of more people there should be space for everyone. And the view is killer. It's on a rise and just far enough away from downtown that, on a clear day, when you look out you can see almost to the other side of the valley. Our side faces south so we should get a lot of natural light," Pat told them. "We just put the papers in today, so we don't know how long it will be until we can move in, but we'll keep all of you informed as we get more information."

Over the next two weeks George and Pat signed contracts with five new clients and moved into the new office. George would go home, drop onto the couch, kick off his shoes, and call Alex. He would relax as they talked about their respective days. Alex was a great support, and George always felt energized after talking with her.

Alex told him the things she was learning about the church and about how things were going at the resort. They started ending their calls with a prayer and both of them commented on the difference that that made on how well they slept.

It was a month and a half since Alex's last visit before George could go to visit her again. Each was anxious to see the other. George was able to leave two hours early on Friday by working frantically that week to clear his calendar. He already had his weekend bag and camera in the car when he left at three.

 George struggled with not to speeding. He put church music in the CD player to help him stay calm, but it just wasn't enough. Suddenly he drove into a microburst. The pavement went from dry to wet, and before George knew what was happening, his car hydroplaned. The car careened out of control, ran off the road and slammed into a tree. The airbag deployed and George felt his nose break with the impact. His head slammed onto the doorframe and he lost consciousness.

"...still unconscious. His responses are good though," a man's voice said.

"Thank you," a woman's voice responded.

George could tell he was lying down, but he felt disinclined to open his eyes or move, feeling like he was pretty banged up. Snippets of the accident flashed though his head. He knew he must be in the hospital and that he was the one they were talking about. He must have given some sort of indication that he was awake because the female voice addressed him.

"Are you awake? Can you open your eyes? I know it might hurt. You had to have stitches on your temple and you broke your nose," the woman said.

Mouth very dry, George managed to say, "Yes, I'm awake. Don't want to open eyes."

"Do you know who you are?" she asked.

"George Albert Hart. I'm in a hospital—car accident," he croaked.

"Very good. Now, can you open your eyes? I know you don't want to, but I need to check your pupils since you've been unconscious for a while now. There, that's good," she said as George did as he was instructed.

A small, bright light was shined into first one eye and then the other. George's headache that had been in the background decided it wanted more attention and became more pronounced.

"Very good, your eyes are responding properly. You'll need to stay in here for about twenty-four hours for observation, but I believe you'll be able to go home soon. Just so you know, I'm the attending physician for the night shift, Dr. Payne. I know, I know. Don't even start. But it could be worse—I could be Dr. Graves," she joked. "Nurse Gomez will check the rest of your vitals and we'll finish up quickly."

The male nurse put a blood pressure cuff around George's arm. "May I close my eyes now? Headache," he said.

"Yes, you may. Do you have anyone we can contact? Your phone was locked so we couldn't check your contact list."

At this George opened his eyes again and tried to sit up.

"Oh my gosh! Alex! I was on my way to visit my girlfriend. Her number is in my phone. Password is 2547, and my parents are Cherish and Kurt, under 'mom'. Tell my parents not to worry, that you're just giving them a heads-up. I'm not sure if Alex will be able to come tonight. If not, it's okay. What time is it?" he asked, closing his eyes again, his newfound energy already expended.

"It's one-twenty a.m.," Dr. Payne said.

"Don't call my parents until the morning then. Or, if you'll let me, I'll call them."

"We'll see if you can. Right now you need to get your rest. We'll notify Alex that you're here, and let you know if she says she'll be coming tonight or in the morning."

The medication that the nurse put into his I.V. kicked in, and George was asleep before he could say anything more.

The next morning George slowly came to consciousness and felt like a sumo wrestler had decided to use him for practice without telling him. He groaned as he moved, feeling like every muscle in his body had been beaten up two or three times over. He wanted to open his eyes, but it hurt too much to even try, so he left them closed. He heard a noise next to him and decided that if Alex were there, it would be worth the pain.

Alex sat slumped in a chair next to the bed, with what looked to be a hospital blanket just about to fall off her lap. He watched through slit eyes as she started to stir.

"Good morning, Sleeping Beauty," he said in a voice just barely stronger than it had been the night before.

At this Alex woke up, looking slightly disoriented for a few seconds before the memory of where she was and why returned.

"Oh, George! You're awake. Are you okay? I mean, I know you must be sore and you're hurt, but are you okay?" she asked, almost panicked.

"Yes, Love, I'm okay. I feel pretty beat up and I have the worst headache of my life, but I'm okay. Boy, aren't you a sight for sore eyes, though. How long have you been here?" he asked.

"George, this is no time to be making jokes. I was scared out of my wits when I got the call last night. I drove right over and have only been here for about two hours. With the adrenaline pumping, I'm not sure how I even got to sleep," she said.

George could see some of the tension leave Alex, but she was still wound up pretty tightly.

149

"Actually this *is* the best time to joke. Helps me think of something besides how much everything I do hurts. Come over here, I want to hold your hand and make sure you really are here. I had dreams about you last night, but I don't really remember what they were. Just that I would try to touch you but you wouldn't be where I put my hand."

Somewhat hesitantly, Alex pulled her chair closer and took George's hand.

"You know, I think my hand is the only part of me that doesn't actually hurt," George commented as his fingers wrapped around her hand. "But all the muscles up my arm hurt like the dickens."

As Alex examined George's face, she carefully brushed his hair off his forehead.

Just then Dr. Payne came in and pushed the curtain away from the end of George's bed.

"Oh, good, you are awake. I tried to tell you last night that she was on her way, but you were kinda out of it so I wasn't sure you'd remember. Head injuries will do that to you. You've got a slight concussion so we're going to keep you for a bit longer. But if all goes well, you should be able to go home tomorrow morning or afternoon at the latest. I'm about to go off duty, so Dr. Christopherson will take over your case. He can be something of a bully, but don't let that get to you. He's a great doctor."

"Thank you, doctor," Alex said. "Have a good day."

"I will. Thank you."

The rest of the day went by rather slowly and painfully for George. Alex was there, constantly looking worried even though he kept reassuring her he was going to be fine. Doctors and nurses came and went, shining light into his eyes, checking his blood pressure, and doing other medical things. At one point he was wheeled to another part of the hospital for a MRI. The doctor came back later to tell him that the MRI looked fine, and that as long as everything stayed the same or got better, he would be released first thing in the morning. It was at this point that a police officer arrived.

"Hi, I'm Officer Knapp. I'd like to get your statement for the accident report. Can you tell me what happened leading up to the accident?"

"I'm not sure if I can give you much detail, it happened so quickly. I was on my way to my girlfriend's place," he said, indicating Alex, "heading north. I couldn't tell the weather was bad because it was so late. One minute I was driving on dry ground, and the next I was on wet ground and the car hydroplaned. I tried to get it under control. I think I was able to take my foot off the gas, but I'm not sure. The next thing I remember is waking up here."

"Do you remember how fast you were going?"

"No. Just that I was trying not to speed. I have an overnight bag and my camera case in the car. I don't know if anyone's looked in the trunk, but I'd like to have them before I leave. I'm guessing the car was totaled."

"We'll get you your things before you leave, and yes, it was totaled. I'm not sure if it will make you feel any better, but the owner of the property where you crashed was just about to have the tree you hit felled. Your hitting it took care of that, though."

"No, doesn't make me feel any better, sorry. I'm really tired. If you don't have any more questions, I think I need to take a nap," George said, yawning.

"No, I think that does it. I certainly hope you feel better soon. I'll have someone bring your things over later today. Good day, ma'am," the officer said.

A couple of hours later a nurse brought George's things to him. Alex left to get some food and go for a walk, returning when George's vitals were being checked again. She still looked anxious even though the doctors and nurses assured her George was going to be fine. After this last check George was given the go-ahead to get up to use the bathroom.

Once he was back in bed George told Alex, "I thought I hurt just lying here, barely moving. Getting up is a hundred times worse, but hopefully that will get better in a day or two."

He instantly regretted his words as he saw Alex tense up even more than she already was.

"Come here, Honey," he said, patting the edge of the bed. "I can tell something is bothering you--you keep tensing up instead

151

of relaxing. I'm not good for hugs right now, but I can hold your hand. Tell me what's wrong."

Alex came over but didn't sit down.

"I—I can't tell you. I love you so much, but I just can't tell you what's wrong. Please, just leave it alone," she begged, the anxiety in her eyes clear to him.

"I'll drop it for now, but you have to promise that once I'm home we'll talk about it, okay?" he said.

"Promise," she whispered reluctantly.

George had to be content with that, but he was still worried.

The next morning, after a final examination, George was pronounced well enough to go home. Alex drove him. Once at his place he took a quick shower, frowning at the bruise on his chest where his seatbelt had stopped him. His nose was doing well although it was still swollen, and he and two black eyes.

After his shower he dressed and checked his mail. There wasn't anything that couldn't wait, so went to bed, more tired than he thought he should be since he had just spent the better, or worse, part of the last day in bed.

He could hear Alex puttering around in the kitchen as he got into bed, and was slightly surprised when she knocked on the door.

"Come in," he said.

Alex came in with a tray of food.

"I thought you might be hungry, so I heated up a can of soup and made a sandwich for you."

"Thank you, Honey. I could use some food."

George sat up and took the tray from Alex, settling it on his lap. She watched him for a minute.

"Should I call Sister Snow or just sleep on the couch? I don't feel right about leaving before tomorrow. I've already called Mrs. Hagerman and she said it's okay if I don't come in until Tuesday."

"Go ahead and sleep on the couch. If you're staying to help me, you can't do that from the Snows' place, although at this point I don't know if there's much you can do to help me other than cooking. There are clean sheets in the hall closet and there might be a pillow, as well.

"I called Pat from the hospital when you stepped out to get some dinner, so he's not expecting me for a day or two. I will need to make arrangements to get a new car, but I'll take care of that tomorrow," George said.

"Well, if you don't need anything else right now, let me know when you're done eating and I'll come get your tray."

George nodded. After he had eaten the sandwich and half of the soup, he called Alex and she took the tray to the kitchen. He lay down and fell asleep.

When George woke up, it was dark outside although the alarm clock showed it was only six. He got up carefully and used the bathroom before venturing into the living room. There he found Alex watching a movie. He sat down at the opposite end of the couch, remembering how Alex had been acting at the hospital and thinking that she might need some space. Once the movie was over George asked Alex what was bothering her.

"Okay, we're back here and you promised to tell me what's bothering you. I had no right to make you promise, so you just tell me when you're ready, okay?"

"Thank you. I really don't feel that I'm ready to talk about it. Will you just hold me for a bit?" she asked.

"Sure, come here."

She snuggled next to him, careful of his bruises, and he held her for several minutes.

"Alex, Honey," he said.

"Yes?"

"I need you to move. My leg where you're leaning against me is falling asleep. I think I need some more food, too."

"Oh, I'm sorry," she said as she moved. "Would you like me to get you something to eat?"

"I'd like to try to do it myself, but thanks. Best way to work out sore muscles is to move around, I've found. But maybe you can help. Are you hungry?"

Looking at her watch she said, "Yes, I am. I didn't realize how late it was."

They went to the kitchen and worked mostly in silence while they made spaghetti and heated up some mixed vegetables.

Once everything was ready and the table set, they sat down. George blessed the food and they started to eat.

After dinner Alex took care of the dishes. George felt tired again so he went back to bed. He slept fitfully, dreaming of the accident and of calling out for Alex but receiving no answer. He finally woke up to light hitting his eyes from the blinds that weren't quite shut all the way.

He went to find Alex. What he found instead made his heart clench. Alex had left a note on the kitchen table.

"Dear George,

This is one of the hardest things I've ever done. I don't think I can see you anymore. Please don't try to contact me, and please believe that I have my reasons. Thank you for all you've done for me.

Alex"

George sat down numbly as he tried to process what he had just read. He felt like he was Alice falling down the rabbit hole. When he finally came to himself, he realized he had been sitting there for about fifteen minutes. He read the letter over again to see if there were any clues as to why she had left like this. Finding none, he disregarded her request that he not contact her and called her. Disappointed that she let the call go to voicemail, he didn't leave a message. She loved him, he knew she did, so he had no idea what had changed her mind about being with him, or even staying friends.

The next week George went about in a fog, trying to work but he unable to focus on anything for very long, trying to figure out the puzzle that was Alex. Finally on Friday he called Mrs. Hagerman and asked her if she knew anything.

"I'm sorry, George. She hasn't told me anything and I tried to get it out of her. She's been moping around, but since she's still doing her job I can't threaten to fire her. She did tell me that if you called to tell you to leave her alone. You didn't have a falling out, did you?"

"No. She just left a note with no explanation as to why she doesn't want to see me. I know she loves me. It was too real for that to be a lie," George said.

"I think she does, too. I would put you through to her, but she's actually not here today. She had a family emergency and flew to Georgia, and I'm not sure when she'll be back. When she does get back, I'll let you know how she seems to be doing," Mrs. Hagerman offered.

"Thank you. I guess that's all I can do for now. Have a good day."

"Oh, I forgot, how are you doing? Alex said you were in an accident last weekend."

"I'm black and blue but doing better, thank you. My car was totaled, though, from kissing a tree that was in the way."

"I'm glad you're doing better. I have to go now. Take care and try not to worry too much. Worrying will only give you ulcers."

"I'll try. 'Bye."

Hearing that Alex seemed to doing just as badly as he was, George was slightly heartened. But George didn't know enough about Alex's family to know whom a family emergency might be for.

He decided to take Mrs. Hagerman's advice and try not to worry, as there was nothing he could do about the situation right then.

The next few weeks kept George so busy that he didn't have time to think about Alex until he got home. For some reason, he and Pat kept on getting new clients or former clients who wanted new advertising done. They decided to have two positions opened for interns, and they quickly found two students who needed some experience for their classes. Showing the interns the ropes and getting them started on their first projects also kept George busy.

At a powwow with George, Pat said, "If business keeps up like this--which we have no way of knowing--we'll need to move to a bigger place by the end of the lease. We'll have hired more people than will fit in here."

George thought about that for a few seconds.

"I think we should try to stay here as long as possible. We have enough space for at least three or four more desks. We might need to re-think how we assign jobs, but I'm pretty sure we can make it work. If we get to the point where we have to move, we'll talk with everyone," George said

George's desk phone rang the following Thursday.

"Hart Advertising, George speaking," he said.

"George, how are you? This is Mrs. Hagerman."

"I'm much better, thank you. How are you?"

"I'm well, thank you. I'm calling to let you know that Alex is back and she's in an even worse funk than when she left. Apparently her uncle just passed away. Do you think you can come up tomorrow or Saturday? The girl just won't tell me what's wrong and I've even tried bullying it out of her," she said in disgust.

"I'll be up. Don't tell Alex I'm coming—I'd like the element of surprise."

"Of course. To make it easier for you, I'll comp you a room. Anything I can do to get Alex straightened out should be worth it. What time should I tell the front desk to expect you?"

"Thank you, Mrs. Hagerman. That would make things much more convenient for me. I'll probably get there about one in the morning on Saturday. If you'll have Alex come in to work, let me know once she's there, I'll come down and talk with her."

"I'll make sure she's here if I have to drag her from her apartment," Mrs. Hagerman promised.

That Friday George started off for Lake Tahoe once again. This time he drove more carefully and got to the resort at five after one. He checked in and went to his room, glad that it was only on the second floor.

At nine George's alarm went off. He got up and ordered room service, wanting to avoid the restaurant where he might accidentally bump into Alex as she was arriving. He showered and dressed. Just after ten Mrs. H. called to let him know that Alex was in and told him how to find her office.

George hung up and went downstairs. At Alex's office door he took a deep breath, exhaled, and then knocked.

"Come in," Alex said. George opened the door. "Just put them on the desk," Alex said without looking up from the paperwork on her desk.

"I'm not bringing anything but a humble heart and a plea to find out why you broke up with me," George said, closing the door. "How was your trip? Mrs. H. said you had a family emergency."

Alex's head snapped up sharply when she realized it was George.

"What are you doing here? I told you not to contact me," she said, looking scared and ready to run.

"First, I wanted to make sure that your family member is okay; I know you don't have a lot of family. Second, I came to get some answers and I don't intend to leave until I get them. Mrs. H. is behind me on this one," he said as he walked over to her and took her cold hands in his.

"My-my uncle passed away. He'd helped raise me. I went to be with him and my aunt. Then he passed away and I stayed for the funeral," she said haltingly.

"I am so sorry to hear that."

"Thank you," Alex replied.

George took a deep breath before starting. He knew that what he had to say needed to be said, but he was not sure of the outcome. He only knew that he had to try to find out what had spooked Alex so much that she broke up with him.

"I came to tell you that I love you and that I know you love me. Everything was fine until I woke up in the hospital. After that you were jittery and evasive. Then you left that note saying you don't want to see me anymore. I don't know what went wrong. Did I do something, not do something? Whatever it is, I can't do anything to try to fix it or to try to understand if you don't tell me what it is. They say anything worth having is worth fighting for, and if I have to fight you to have you, I'll do it. I love you too much to just let you walk away."

Alex looked down at her hands and George waited. After a few minutes she looked up, the scared look in her eyes magnified by the tears that threatened to overflow. She took a deep breath and gripped his hands, her hands shaking slightly.

"I've never told anyone about this. You know how I told you that my brother died? He and my parents died in a car accident. After that I went to live with my aunt and uncle. They're good people, but they weren't prepared to take me in. My uncle and my dad were brothers and they'd had something of a falling out years before I was born. But they were the only relatives I had that could take me, so they took me in. They didn't have any children of their own, and didn't want any. They gave me all the

157

physical things that I needed, but they were never very good at showing me any affection. There were rules that were to be followed and behavior that was expected. I knew from the beginning that they weren't happy to have me, but because I knew that the alternative was to go into foster care, I did all I could to make them not regret that they let me live with them. When they first took me in I tried every now and then to hug them, but I could tell that they didn't really like it, so I stopped. By the time I graduated, I almost never talked with them, other than to tell them things they needed to know. I was very glad to move out and be able to have my own place where I didn't feel unwanted.

"Being with you and your family has brought back some of the things I'd forgotten about from before my parents died. I'll always be grateful for that. But it's also reminded me of how lonely I've been since then. I didn't make friends easily, and the ones I did make ended up moving away, or we moved. You're the first person I've felt close to since my parents died that I thought cared about how I felt."

"That still doesn't explain why you ran," he said.

She took a deep breath and let it out. "It was because of me that my parents and brother died. It's my fault. It was Christmas time and I wanted to go to the wedding of a family friend who had a daughter my age. The daughter and I had become friends the year before and I wanted a chance to visit with her again. I talked my parents into going. We were driving through the night so we could spend as much time as possible there, and we drove into a storm. We were driving along a mountainside and a mudslide pushed us off the road. The mud broke the windows on the passenger side, killing my mom and brother right away. The car slammed into a tree on driver's side, and Dad hit his head on the door too hard. I was in the back seat asleep while all this was happening. When I woke up, we were against the tree and there wasn't anything I could do. Mud was all over the car, inside and out, and I was trapped. The tree was blocking my door so I couldn't open it, and mud was coming in the other side. I screamed and cried but there wasn't anyone who could hear me. I was lucky because there had been a car driving just close enough behind us to see us get pushed off the road without getting caught in the slide. They came down to see how bad it was and they were able to get me out of the car. There wasn't anything anyone could do for the rest of my family.

"When I got the call that you'd been hurt coming to visit me, it was like losing my family all over again. You were coming to see me. If it hadn't been for that, you would have been fine. I don't ever want to lose anyone I love again, so I can't be with you or your family. I don't know if I could take it if you died because of me!" she said, pulling her hands out of his and covering her face, sobbing.

George pulled her to him, sitting on the floor to hold her. He let her cry for several minutes until he could tell she was starting to calm down. He now understood why she had been so scared, and he felt his heart break that no one had thought to talk with her about this before.

"Alex, Sweetheart, thank you for telling me this. It helps me to understand some of your reactions and comments better. I care about you and the pain you've suffered. I hurt when I see the pain in your eyes. I want to laugh when I see you happy. But most of all, I want to see you at peace, at peace with yourself, and at peace with your past.

"It's not your fault that they died, it really isn't. You did not cause the rain or the mudslide. You had no way of knowing that by sitting behind your dad that you, and not your brother, would live. Your parents made the choice to go, they didn't have to. Sometimes things like this happen. I know. It happened to Jane and me."

Alex lifted her head at this and George gently wiped the tears off her cheek and brushed her hair back behind her ear.

"What do you mean, it happened to you and Jane?" she asked in a voice raw from crying so hard.

"One year when I was in college I decided to go home with one of my roommates who lived in Colorado. We wanted to go skiing there. Jane sneaked out to go to a Christmas party that Mom and Dad had told her she couldn't go to because there wasn't going to be any parental supervision. When Mom and Dad found out she had gone, Dad went to get her. While he was out a blizzard came up and he slid off the road. He was stuck in his car with only his jacket and an old blanket to keep him warm. The place where he slid off the road was at the edge of a culvert where the snow was really deep. By the time Dad was found he was suffering from hypothermia. When they got him to the hospital, the doctor didn't know if it was too late or not. They were, of course, able to revive him, but he was in a coma for a couple days recovering.

"For a long time Jane felt that it was her fault that Dad almost died, because she had disobeyed. I felt guilty because I hadn't been there. Over time we were able to realize that while our actions had consequences, we didn't *cause* the blizzard, nor did we make the truck go off the road. If I had been there, I could just as easily have been caught in the blizzard with him or on my own. You asked me before if I believe we have control over our lives. I believe we are given the freedom to make choices, but we aren't able to choose what happens because of those choices. Heavenly Father lets us make mistakes. If Dad had died, it would have been a lot harder for us to overcome, but we would eventually have been okay because Christ's atonement makes it possible for us to find peace and forgiveness. He suffered so that He can understand all that we go through-- our little hurts and our big ones, our guilt over something that was our fault and our guilt over something that we only thought was our fault. If we turn to Him and understand that we can be forgiven, even if only by ourselves, He can help us heal. He can help us find peace and comfort. I love you and I don't blame you at all for what happened to your family. I know that the Lord doesn't hold you accountable for this either. If you can't believe this yet for yourself, believe that I know it to be true.

"And we rarely know when our time is up. If you don't allow yourself to love or be loved, you miss out on so much joy. Yes, there's sorrow, too, when someone we love is no longer with us, but that is part of life, and who are we to say that it should not be so? Everyone dies, but through Christ all will be made alive again because He was resurrected. He paved the way for us in life and in death as we, too, will be resurrected some day."

Alex looked at George for a long time while what he said sank in. He could tell there was a battle raging inside her between the guilt she had carried most of her life and his words, which absolved her of this guilt.

"If you'd like, we can say a prayer to help you understand that Heavenly Father loves you and doesn't blame you for this. I know it might take a while for you to feel at peace, but this is a place to start," he offered.

Mutely Alex nodded and readied herself for the prayer.

George prayed that Alex would feel the love that her Father in Heaven had for her, that she would understand that what happened to her parents was not her fault, that she should and could forgive herself for something that she had had no control over. After closing the prayer George sat with his arms folded and head bowed for several more minutes as he said his own prayer, asking that he might be able to help Alex understand the truth of what he had told her, and asking that she would accept his love.

When he finally looked up, Alex's eyes were shining--not with tears, but with the Spirit. George knew everything would be all right.

"I can feel it. I feel what you've said is true. While you were saying the prayer, I felt like I was in my mom's arms and she was telling me it was time to let go, to not blame myself anymore, that everything was the way it was meant to be. Thank you. Thank you for loving me and wanting to help me. I don't think anyone else has cared about me as much as you have since my parents.

"Writing that letter was one of the hardest things I've ever done because I felt like I was ripping out a part of me, a part that I didn't know I had. But I felt that if I didn't push you away and you did die, that I would die, too. You have helped make me whole. Please don't go away again, I don't think I could stand it. You've helped me find the strength that I need," she said.

"I have no intentions of leaving you. Not for long, anyway. One of the things we believe as a Church is that by being married by the proper Priesthood authority, we can be joined together for eternity," he said as he pulled a small box out of his pocket and then opened it. "Alex, would you do me the honor of marrying me and being my wife? I, too, feel like I'm less than whole when you're not around. I'm tired of your being all the way up here and my being in L.A. Will you help make me whole?"

Alex had been so intent on what George was saying that she hadn't yet looked at the box. Once he finished speaking she looked and saw a beautiful gold band with a simple square-cut emerald. George took the ring from the box and held it at her ring finger.

"Alex, will you marry me?" he asked again, waiting for her to look at him.

"Yes, George, I will marry you and we can both be whole," she said, tears of joy trembling on the ends of her eyelashes. She slipped her finger into the ring.

Epilogue
A year and a half later...

"Are you ready?" George asked Alex as he took her hand.

"Ready as I'll ever be," she replied, running her hand down the antique lace on the skirt of her wedding dress.

George pushed open the door of the Boise temple and the two walked out into the warmth of the summer day. As their friends and family caught sight of them, Jane started snapping pictures and everyone else cheered. George and Alex walked down to the people who loved them and who had helped bring this day about.

It had been a quick year since the bishop had married them, but it had been a great year. George and Alex had gotten to know one another better, and Alex had gotten to know the Lord better. It hadn't been a perfect first year, but it had been perfectly wonderful. George knew even more strongly now that he was supposed to be with Alex and that he never wanted to be without her. Her warm spirit, love of life, and eagerness to learn about her role in life made him love her more each day. He prayed fervently that their love would continue to grow, and with that growing, their understanding of their Heavenly Father's love for them.

He looked at Alex, his bride for the second time. This was one of the days he'd looked forward to all his life. He could not wait to get to the others...

Recipes

Here are a couple recipes from the book. The mint lemonade is from one of my Young Woman leaders, the macaroni salad is my mom's (love you Mummy!), and the breakfast burrito is my own. Feel free to play with them and make them your own, but either way, I hope you enjoy them as much as I do.

Mint Lemonade

2 ½ c sugar
2 c water
A handful fresh mint leaves (several varieties to choose from if you want to grow your own)
10-12 oz each frozen orange juice and lemonade concentrate
Water to mix w/ punch base

Make syrup of:
2 1/2 c sugar
2 c water
Boil 10 min. Turn off heat and add a handful of washed fresh mint and let sit until cool. Remove mint. Mix syrup with 10 each frozen orange juice and lemonade concentrate. Concentrate comes in 12 oz can, so you could use the whole can if you want to. This is the base. Store in fridge or freezer.

To mix, use 1 part punch base w/ 5 parts water or to taste.
You can also heat up about 6-8 oz after mixed and add about a TBS of honey.

Macaroni Salad

12-16 oz salad, shells, elbow or your choice pasta cooked, drained, and cooled.

Dressing:
1 cup or so Miracle Whip (yes, it matters)
1-2 cans tuna, undrained
¼ cup sweet relish
1 TBS lemon juice

Seasonings as desired:
Celery salt, parsley flakes, seasoning salt, onion salt, garlic salt,
Mrs. Dash, Paprika, salt, pepper, turmeric, etc.
1 can diced beets, drained and rinsed (optional)
6 eggs, hard-boiled, chopped—reserve one egg, sliced, for garnish

Combine in a big bowl all of the dressing ingredients holding out
one sliced egg for garnish. Add Pasta and stir gently until all pasta
is well coated, add more Miracle Whip if needed. Garnish with the
sliced egg and sprinkle with some paprika. Refrigeration for a few
hours blends the flavors better before serving.

Breakfast Burrito

1 strip of bacon cut in half (I like bacon with some fat on it as it
helps grease the pan)
1 button mushroom cut in slices (can use pre-sliced or use an egg
slicer to cut a whole one-optional)
2 eggs or equal egg substitute
Small handful of uncooked spinach (optional)
Small amount of bell pepper cut into small chunks (or whatever
kind of pepper you like-optional)
Small handful of shredded cheese of choice (I use Mexi-blend, but
hard cheeses are good, too)
1 large tortilla
Refried beans
Sour cream, guacamole, and/or Ranch dressing whatever you
prefer (optional)

On medium heat (adjust for your stove and pan), in a small skillet
cook bacon and mushrooms. While those are cooking smear refried
beans onto center of tortilla and sprinkle on cheese. Scramble the
eggs. Once you have cooked the bacon almost completely on the
first side flip bacon/mushrooms over, pour in eggs and cover. As
soon as you put the eggs in, using a microwave safe plate, heat
tortilla for 1 minute. Once that's done, put on toppings of choice.
Put handful of spinach on eggs when eggs are almost done
cooking-turn OFF heat. Once spinach has softened, fold in half,
pressing down on it with spatula to make sure any egg not cooked

is pushed to the outside. When it looks like the all the egg is cooked (30-90 seconds), flip over and let finish cooking for another minute if it needs it. Place on top of toppings. Wrap like a burrito and enjoy!